BEST BONDAGE EROTICA

BEST BONDAGE EROTICA

Edited by

Alison Tyler

Published in the United States by Cleis Press Inc.,
P.O. Box 14684, San Francisco, California 94114.
Printed in the United States.
Cover design: Scott Idleman
Text design: Karen Quigg
Cleis Press logo art: Juana Alicia
First Edition.
10 9 8 7 6 5 4 3 2

Acknowledgments

For unwavering support and unconventional sweetness, I thank Violet Blue, Spencer C., Eliza Castle, Judy Cole, Alex D., Jeannine Laddomada, Mike Ostrowski, Barbara Pizio, Thomas S. Roche, Jimmy S., Kerri Sharp, and of course—Felice, Don, and Frédérique. I couldn't have done it without you.

CONTENTS

ix **Introduction**

1 **Moving** M. Christian
11 **The Perfect O** Cara Bruce
18 **Bad Girls in Bondage** Thomas S. Roche
28 **Blushing Beauty** Emilie Paris
34 **A Betting Man** Sage Vivant
46 **The First Pinch** Michele Zipp
54 **Strictly Business** Mark Williams
61 **Restraining Order** Dante Davidson
65 **Never Say Never** Rachel Kramer Bussel
73 **Home Entertainment** Felix D'Angelo
79 **Good Things Come** Iris N. Schwartz
84 **Melinda** Mitzi Szereto
99 **For Emphasis** Becky Chapel
105 **Caged** Derek Hill
110 **Six Persimmons** Helena Settimana
119 **Safeway** Marilyn Jaye Lewis
132 **Shock Therapy** N. T. Morley
158 **Cops and Robbers** KC
165 **Selling Point** Carl Kennedy
175 **Hard Core** Alex Mendra
188 **The Morning After...** Alison Tyler

195 **About the Authors**
200 **About the Editor**

Love is a kind of warfare. —OVID

Love is a fiend, a fire, a heaven, a hell,
where pleasure, pain, and sad
repentance dwell.

—RICHARD BARNFIELD

Introduction

When I'm working hard, I like to tell people that I'm tied to my desk. Because of the genre of writing I work in, this comment always wins me a chuckle, and an extra-long, sideways glance. Am I intentionally making a double entendre, or am I *really* tied to my desk? You can see it, can't you—his wallet chain wrapped around my slim ankles, keeping me firmly fixed at my computer when I have an encroaching deadline? Nice image, right? And you'll never know for sure, now, will you?

But I must admit, for this collection, I needed no added incentive to put in long hours reading submissions. That's because bondage is my favorite way to play—I adore *all* forms of bondage—from the seduction of a simple set of stainless steel handcuffs to the most intricate, indecipherable rope knots, to the hard-core quality of chains.

Even way back at the very beginning, I liked being held in place by my wrists. That spot on the inside of the wrist, in the delicate curve, is my most sensitive region. I used to hold up my wrists to my lovers and say, "Kiss here. Touch *here,*" long before I realized that I wanted even more than that. I wanted to be captured in strong hands, in firm bonds, unable to get free.

When I was eighteen, I worked in Los Angeles on an entertainment weekly. My editor took an extra interest in my education, far beyond the scope of teaching me how to structure an exciting news story. Alexander bought me music he thought I should own—"*Every* girl needs a copy of Roxy Music's *Avalon,*" he declared knowingly. He took me shopping for naughty knickers before I went out on dates. And he shared sexually explicit stories with me, pretending that he was simply trying to expand my sheltered world.

My favorite tantalizing tale focused on how he'd held a girlfriend down in bed, his large hands firm on her fine wrists, elongating her body by holding her hands over her head. I was naive—too naive to know that he was putting the moves on me—but I understood one thing for certain: that image turned me on. To this day, the mental picture remains in my head whenever I think of bondage as an erotic subject. Because in my opinion, the concept of bondage begins in the mind, expanding to contain all ranges of restraint—with bare hands, ties, rope, belts, fur-lined cuffs, silk scarves, serious chains, or even simply a command to keep oneself still. You'll find an assortment of these genres within this collection, from the unusual "Moving" by multitalented M. Christian, to the delicious "Melinda" by Mitzi Szereto. N. T. Morley pokes fun at couples' therapy in the vibrantly creative "Shock Therapy" and Alex Mendra tells the tale of an eco-challenge gone bad in his ferocious tale "Hard Core."

As this is a "best of" collection, several stories have appeared in other anthologies or on websites, but you'll also find a wide assortment of "virgin" pieces, stories that have never been published before and are presented here as delicious newcomers to the bondage banquet.

So now's the time to find a quiet spot, relax, and bind yourself down with a nice, kinky book. And when people ask you what you've been up to, smile as you reply that you were all tied up this weekend....

Alison Tyler
March 2003

Moving

M. Christian

"Don't move," she said.

"That's it?" I said.

"That's it. That's it, exactly: Don't move."

"Right now?" Smiling.

She returned it. "Right now—but get comfortable first."

"Isn't that sort of counterproductive?"

She tapped the tip of my nose. "Comedian. Don't worry—you'll get an experience."

"But not a moving one, eh?"

The smile stayed, but her words were serious: "Great experiences are always moving—but not vice versa. Not at all."

At least Sybil's basement was warm.... No, that's not it. *Dungeon:* that's what she'd called it, though I still couldn't think of it that way. Dungeon: bricks, rats, iron bars, and *The Man in the Iron Mask*. Who was in that anyway, Lon Chaney? Errol Flynn? Jose Ferrer? I'll have to look it up later.

A dungeon certainly wasn't a basement rec room in the Avenues, the perpetually foggy ocean side of San Francisco.

No bricks, no iron bars, no rats—as far as I could see. But if that's what Sybil wanted to call it, that's what I should probably call it, too.

Golden-yellow, low-pile shag carpeting. A heavy table covered in black leather. A pine chest with a latch and padlock—closed and locked. It certainly wasn't a place that Lon Chaney, Errol Flynn or Jose Ferrer would have been scared of—hell, Errol would have probably been overjoyed at the sight, knowing his reputation.

But I wasn't Errol—or Jose or Lon, or even Brendan Fraser—and I'd be lying if I said I wasn't at least nervous. It wasn't that I didn't trust Sybil, but this was something new. For me, sex had always been about a cock (mine), tits and pussies—not whips, chains and "Yes, Mistress." But that's what it was for Sybil. At least she understood my trepidation, thus the padlock on her war chest.

What am I doing here? This wasn't the first time I'd thought that, walking in the door to her place. The response was the same as it had always been: this is part of her life, and I want to be part of her life, too.

But there was something else—bing!—right in front of my face: sure I wanted to stay in good graces with Sybil, but there was something else as well. *Face it,* I told myself, *you just want to see why this isn't a rec room but a dungeon.* I wanted to get it.

"Ready?" she asked.

"Rip roarin' to do absolutely nothing, that is," I said, smiling as always.

"Get comfy. You don't want to cramp up," she said. In a bow to my nervousness she wasn't wearing any of her S/M gear, the leather and latex she'd showed me in the dark depths of her closet, but rather a comfy yellow bathrobe. She still was damned sexy—a beautifully full, round woman with hair dark as night and flickering amber eyes—and, looking at her, the last thing I wanted to do was play her game. It took a huge effort not to just part that robe, cup her breasts, run a thumb over her nipples—but a promise was a promise.

It was also hard, or rather I should say I was also hard, because I definitely was that—because she'd asked me to, and then I did, strip down. I hopped up onto the table, my cock slapping back and forth against my thighs, and tried to work myself into a comfortable position.

After a few minutes I thought I'd found it. "Okay," I said. "I'm all set to do nothing."

"You said that," she said, tightening the tattered yellow sash around her waist. "Now look me in the eyes."

"Yes, Mistress," I said, curbing the mischief I felt tickling my voice.

She frowned—and I felt suddenly, deeply sad. "Don't say that unless you mean it. I'm serious."

"Sorry," I said, opening my hands in supplication.

She looked at me for a moment. "Okay." She took a deep breath. "You do the same, take a couple of deep slow breaths: in, out, in, out. Think about your body, the position you're sitting in. If it doesn't feel good then move."

I breathed, feeling my chest rise and fall. I moved my leg a bit, then my right arm.

"When it feels good, when it feels right, then nod and we'll start. It's a real simple game: just don't move—try and keep the same position as long as you can."

"Hmm.... How do I win?"

"Win? Sweetie, this isn't a win/lose kind of game." She kissed the tip of my nose and I smiled despite myself. Then she looked at me thoughtfully for a long minute. "You know, there might very well be a way to win—but I'm not going to tell you how. You've got to figure that out for yourself. Now, are you ready?"

What the hell was that about? I thought. "Ready as I'll ever be."

"Good. Now start: Don't say anything, don't nod. Don't move."

I didn't say anything, I didn't nod, and I didn't move. We started.

There were rules. For something that wasn't a game, it seemed to have a lot of them: breathing was okay, blinking was okay, involuntary movement was okay, but anything like a conscious twitch or jerk was right out—game over, thank you for playing, here's your complimentary Turtle Wax and a copy of the home game. Thinking of that, the game almost ended before it began, an image dancing through my mind of a two-point-five nuclear family sitting down around a Parker Brothers game of S/M and spinning the punishment wheel. "Uh-oh, Bobby, you drew the Golden Showers card—" But I fought a smirk, locking down my face.

Sybil, meanwhile, sat down on the chest and watched me. She was so pretty. Watching her watch me, a thought flickered through my mind: With a view like this, who cares about moving?

Distantly, I was aware that my cock hadn't gone down: it was still gently throbbing against my thigh.

I blinked.

Then I wondered, still looking at my lover, what was I supposed to do now? The rules of the game were easy enough, but what was the damned point? Was I supposed to make her feel good by obeying her? "Yes, Mistress; no, Mistress; right away, Mistress." That could make anyone feel good—having a humble little slave—but what the hell would I get out of it, aside from a nasty cramp?

When I agreed to play Sybil's game I knew it could be weird, but, hell, I loved her—or at least I thought I did. But this part of her life was something that baffled me, and after a minute of immobility, it still did. Something was niggling at the back of my stock-still noggin: I didn't want to be a pet, a slave, a subservient little twit who'd follow her around, wipe her ass, or who knew what. That idea pissed me off.

I wanted to move, to say "Fuck this!" and get up and walk away. I wanted to break her spell, smash it up and get the hell out of there. It wasn't something I'd thought of when I agreed to play Sybil's game, but sitting there, frozen, it made my face burn. I'm not one of those "top dog" guys, but I sure as shit didn't want to be a whipped one.

Then I thought of something else and I fought to keep a sneer down again: one finger. I wanted to lift just one finger on the hand she couldn't see. She wouldn't know, but I would. There was something juicy in that, a little victory in our battle of "play." When the game was over she would think she'd had a victory when I had really won—and I'd get to smile my secret little smile as she came out the big, bad, Mistress.

I felt my hand, behind me on the warm leather. I was sitting on the edge of the table, one hand to the side, one hand to the back. The one in the back. That one. My left. Maybe the first finger, perhaps the second?

The birdie digit I decided was too rude, too harsh for my subtle little gesture of defiance.

Have you ever thought about moving a part of your body before you actually move it? It's weird, putting consciousness into something you often don't even think about. I felt a tension in my hand, my finger (the first one, if you're curious); the muscles, tendons, tissues and all that wet, squishy stuff change from not moving to starting-to-move. The will was there, definitely, and my body was prepared, absolutely, but then something really interesting happened.

Nothing—that's what happened. Or didn't happen, I didn't know for sure. But I do know that I didn't move, not at all, not even my finger. The room—warm, if not hot—was suddenly chilly and a parade of goose bumps ran up and down my spine, arms and thighs. I remained frozen, immobile.

Why? Thoughts in my head, thumping together like idea bumper cars; weird feelings; odd impressions—and something else. Have you ever suddenly realized that your body was doing something you didn't ask it to do—some part of yourself that you normally have to tell to perform acting on its own? I have, because that's what happened.

My cock, you see, was still hard—rock hard, steel hard, very damned hard. I was angry, or had just been angry, and the one thing that usually doesn't happen when I get angry is staying hard. I shrink, shrivel, get small—you name it, that's what happens, negative erection. But that didn't happen. Frozen for Sybil, my cock was still hard. No, that's not quite right. I'd been hard before (my dick pulsed against my thigh) but now, still not moving, I was incredibly hard.

Sybil, watching me, smiled and winked.

I don't think I've ever been as hard as that—but I certainly hope I will be again. It felt like a deep part of me, somewhere down below my belly button, my guts, my soul even, was happy at this situation. Very, very happy.

But that was way down, cock-response deep, but at the top of it all, in my brain, something else was ringing loud and long: why?

I still didn't know Sybil's "why"—not really. I'd guessed, but I didn't know. That wasn't what was bugging me. Why didn't I move? Why didn't I get up and leave?

Because that's what you've always done, I heard a voice saying clearly in my mind, coming from down there in my guts, somewhere near my soul.

Goose bumps. Big, obvious, goose bumps. I didn't care so much that I was thinking to myself in a new voice, that I'd possibly had a psychotic break, or that I'd been telepathically contacted by beings Not of This Earth, but rather that what that voice said was right. It wasn't something I'd considered before, but hearing it said as I tried to stay as still as possible was frightening—because it was true.

I liked to laugh. Not that I was jolly, or good-spirited, but that everything seemed laughable to me. I giggled and guffawed at the world, seeing the billions and billions that lived on earth—or ever lived for that matter—as suckers, idiots. I didn't believe in anything, I was just another rat in a maze, a moron on a treadmill.

Lifting a finger, cheating at my lover's game: that was so like me. Anything serious, deep, or possibly meaningful was a joke—on everyone.

A joke on you—was that me, was that beyond me, was that somewhere to the left of my soul? I didn't move, but I did: inside, dropping through layers of mind and memory. Pieces of myself floated by my consciousness: birthday traumas, schoolyard pain, moments of clarity and what I thought to be understanding.

I wanted to laugh, but not like I had before. I felt the muscles of my face start to pull and stretch into a grin but I stopped them cold. No movement. None at all. Paralysis. But inside I moved a lot: looking back on my life, looking down and through myself, I realized that I didn't have anything. I was good at things, but never very good at anything. I moved towards things—work, avocations, even love—but I never got close. I stopped just short, never stepping beyond. Giving anything my all would mean stepping out beyond my smirking safety zone.

My leg cramped but I tried to ignore it. Pain flared there, a pulsing new kind of discomfort, but I tried to push it away. It was very important that I not move, not even a little bit.

My eyes were dry but I didn't want to blink. Blinking was movement and movement would mean losing the game. Then

I remembered the game allowed that kind of thing, so I carefully, slowly blinked. It felt good, but I vowed not to do it again—or at least not often.

What had I done in my life? I could have done so much more, I realized. My life suddenly seemed shallow—what had I ever done except laugh a lot? I remembered hearing that a friend of mine in college had written a novel—and for some reason that struck me as pathetic. He'd spent night after night working on something that would probably never see the light of day, or even if it did it would vanish from the stands in a week or two. A friend from high school had been all around the world, visiting the Dalai Lama, watching when the Wall came down in Berlin; I giggled that she'd spent all that time and money and come away with nothing but memories and some snapshots.

My lower back started to ache. It felt like a slug of heavy metal had been slapped against my spine. I so wanted to straighten up, stretch, listen to the music of my bones realigning themselves. But I didn't. I didn't move. I was frozen. In bondage. I was in bondage and so I couldn't, wouldn't move.

What have you done? What have you accomplished?

I'd had girlfriends, women I thought I might—kinda, sorta—love, but they hadn't lasted. They'd wanted to talk, to think about the future, I'd just wanted to have fun. How many had there been? One of them, a fun little redhead named Cheryl, had gotten married—and I remembered laughing at how ridiculous she was, standing up there making her vows in front of the world when—more than likely—she and her husband would be talking to divorce lawyers in a year or two.

What have I done? The answer was not hard—not hard except that I didn't want to say it, or think it, because it came up zero. Nothing. I laughed a lot, and that was all. I wanted to cry. Shame and self-pity surged through me. I wanted Sybil—who was still looking at me with her deep amber eyes—to hold me while my sorrow flowed out. I wanted her to make it all better. She was right there in front of me, filling my vision—and I loved her.

But I didn't cry. Crying would mean moving, would mean that some part of my body had moved and I had failed. I didn't want to screw this up. I wanted to make this happen, to win this game. I wanted to feel good and, right along with that, I wanted Sybil to feel good about me.

My body was a knot. Pain rolled up and through my muscles, tendons, and even—I swear—my bones. My cock was still strong and hard; it hadn't changed at all during my inward movements. I thought about it as I sat there in bondage: how I wanted to touch it, to wrap my hand around it and enjoy its hardness. I wanted Sybil to see and admire it. I wanted to share it with her—to make love to her as we had before—but I also wanted her to see what had happened to me, to see that for the first time in my entire life, I was trying.

I'm trying my best. I will not move. I will not move. I will do this. I want to feel that I've done something special here today, I want to feel pride in an accomplishment—and I want Sybil to understand that.

My legs ached. My back ached. My hand felt like it would never move again. Minutes? No, it felt like I had spent hours in immobility. I wanted to blink again, but didn't. My eyes were dry, burning. I held my breath, because breathing was movement. It was okay, according to the rules, but not according to my rules. I didn't want to win by the rules.

I wanted to do better than the rules.

My head started to swim and for a heart-pounding minute I thought I'd moved, that my head had tipped forward, and I felt a surge of panic and shame. But then I realized that I was still where I'd been: still frozen in place.

My cheeks felt strange. Had I moved? Had I failed? I hoped, prayed that I hadn't moved. I didn't want to—

I wanted to rise up, to move beyond what and where I'd been before.

Sybil got up, walked towards me—the expression on her face new, unusual. I hadn't seen her like this before. I'd seen her laugh, cry, orgasm, sigh, get angry, but this was new—was this disappointment? I felt deep sorrow that I might have failed her. I hoped not. I really, honestly hoped not.

I didn't move.

Her hand went up to my cheek—her touch like an electric shock—and I expected my whole body to jump at the contact. But it didn't. I didn't move. Not an inch, not a little bit, not at all. I didn't move.

"Sweetheart," she said, bending down to look into my eyes. "Sweetheart," she said again. "Thank you—thank you so much. You've done what I wanted and more."

That look on her face, and there in her eyes. Something new, something I wanted more and more of. Something I'd been missing for all those years, something I'd given up on finding: respect.

"Thank you, Mistress," I said, the tears now pouring down my cheeks.

"Thank you so much."

The Perfect O

Cara Bruce

I never knew I liked pain, or how much I liked it. I've had fantasies and my bookshelves are lined with romance novels involving Victorian classrooms and harsh punishments. But I didn't *know*. What I have always known is my love of jewelry. It started out when I was little as a fascination with my mothers'. I would sit for hours holding her long earrings up to my tiny lobes, shaking my head so they would brush against my seven-year-old shoulders. Then I became obsessed with the junk they sold in the dollar store at the mall, fluorescent parrots, rubber oranges—anything bright and fancy attached to a metal post. Every special event in my life has been marked by the gift of earrings: topaz for my eighteenth birthday, aquamarine from my first serious boyfriend, diamonds for my college graduation and a pair of black pearls from my grandmother when she passed away.

I still have every pair. Mark, my last lover, bought me a beautiful mahogany jewelry box, lined in deep brown velvet and speckled with tiny holes for the thin posts of my treasures. Small, pull-out boxes ran along the bottom—the perfect place for safe storage of rusting faux silver and chipped gold. After Mark left I thought of putting the box back in my closet with the pop-up white ballerina box my father bought me years ago for my sixteenth birthday. It was the typical gift of a father with no concept of what a sixteen-year-old girl needs or wants, a father still desperately trying to clutch on to the passing away of youth, hers and his, with a twirling, plastic figurine. But then I opened Mark's mahogany box, ran my finger over the shiny remnants of my life, and realized what many women before me have tearfully accepted: just because the men are rotten doesn't mean their gifts are.

I didn't think that Kyle, the man I had been seeing for the past three months, had ever noticed that my ears were pierced. So the night I met him for a drink and he tenderly ran his fingertips over my tiny, silver hoops, I was pleasantly surprised. Kyle was what my mother would call "a real catch." He had no particularly bad habits, dressed well, was gainfully employed and naturally good-looking. It was enough to make me wary and I was beginning to grow fearful that he was so perfect he would soon grow dull.

Kyle ordered us another round of drinks. He seemed distracted, fidgeting, glancing at the clock, tapping his fingers, and adjusting his seat. His behavior made me nervous, typical of a man who has something to tell you but doesn't quite know how to put it into words. Finally I had to say something. If I was going to be dealt a blow I wanted to meet it head-on.

"Kyle, what's on your mind?" I said, forcing him to look into my eyes.

He took a moment before he sighed and said, "Your earrings."

"My earrings? You don't like them?" This was not what I expected.

"No, no, they're fine." He fumbled in his briefcase for a moment and brought out a plain brown paper bag, which he slid across the table to me. I opened it up and withdrew a glossy magazine. On the cover was a gorgeous woman wearing an expression of unbridled lust. I opened the slick pages and was met by various shots of women pierced—in every possible location. I flipped the pages silently—my heart beating faster and my crotch growing wet. I looked up at Kyle and comprehension flooded me. His gaze was steadfast and even though I had never known these hoops to hang anywhere but from my ears, I knew I was about to.

I placed the magazine back in its wrapper and instead of returning it to him I slipped it into my purse.

"Let's get out of here," I whispered.

We drove in silence to his house. The faint evening drizzle pattered against the top of his car before it exploded into rain as we pulled into the driveway. We made a dash for the door, dripping as we entered the front hallway. Without a word Kyle led me upstairs to his bedroom. I was nervous. My palms were sweaty and my cunt was throbbing. I began to ask him a question but he motioned with a finger for me to be quiet. He stood me in the center of his room and took a neatly-wrapped gift box off the top of his dresser.

Inside lay a single needle.

As I slowly brought my palm up to examine the object more closely, my heart seemed to stop. He began to look a little uncertain.

"That's okay, isn't it? I went to the piercing shop and asked about the gauge. That's what they told me to get."

"No," I murmured, turning the delicate instrument in my hand, "it's fine."

He smiled, instantly relieved. He placed his arms on my shoulders and gently massaged them. Then, without another word, he began to unbutton my blouse. I felt light-headed and my legs were weak. He slipped the white cotton over my shoulders and stood staring at the clasp-in-front white bra, slightly padded and frayed at the edges. I was embarrassed. If only I had known, I would have bought some new lingerie.

He took a deep breath and unhooked it, slowly, reverently. I was afraid to breathe. But he slipped it off, and smiled.

"Perfect," he whispered, and took a step back to examine these two mounds that I have carried with me my entire life without ever having heard the word *perfect* used to describe them. My breath came back and without a single touch my clit sprang to life.

He was like an enraptured schoolboy, gently rubbing his forefinger over the brown nipple, which had already hardened from its sudden exposure to fresh air.

I closed my hand tight around the needle and moaned. In that moment all hope for my nipples' virginity was gone. He bent down and kissed me, his strong mouth parting mine just enough to allow his tongue to slip tenderly across my teeth. Our bodies remained slightly apart and it took all of my willpower to keep from pulling him close to me and pressing his pelvis against my aching cunt.

"Sit down," he said, moving away and disappearing through the bathroom door.

I had not known I was one for pain.

"Why don't you take off your clothes and get comfortable?" he called. My body moved without thought, unzipping my skirt, rolling down my stockings; trembling, quivering scared...and wanting.

He came back in, naked except for a pair of white boxer shorts that showed the line of his erect cock pushing against the thin fabric.

"The alcohol," he said, and held up a bottle and cotton swabs like a track star with a trophy.

He came over and knelt before me, placing his toys upon

the bedside table. I sighed as he gently kissed the point where my calf began to curve. His mouth worked its way up along the soft inside of my leg, pausing on my thigh. He parted my legs slowly—forcing me to bite my lip with anticipation—and buckled my ankles to leather restraints that must have been previously secured to the wooden bedposts.

I jolted at the feel of the cool buckles against my skin. "It will be easier if you can't move," he explained calmly. He reached up and took my right arm, bringing it to the post above me. Buckles were secured against my right wrist, then my left. Not only were the restraints keeping me still, they were making me terribly aroused. I sat on the edge of his bed: wet, wanting, and spread out for his needle.

He reached up to uncurl my hand that was still clenched around the instrument. Then, with careful precision he wiped it clean with the alcohol. He blew on my nipples. They were so hard they looked as if they could have been popped off by a simple flick of his thumb. I gasped. He drew the soaked swab across and smiled as they amazingly grew another millimeter. He looked into my eyes, "Just relax," he whispered.

I felt the needle as soon as it touched the edge of my breast. He was teasing me, tracing the curve of my falling bosom with the cool metal before bringing it to the edge of my hard bud. I moved against the restraints but they were too tight.

"Relax," he said, "I'm just going to push the needle in, leave it for a moment, pull it out and replace it with the hoops. Then, once they are in, I'm going to kiss you all over. I'm going to make circles on your clit with my tongue. I promise you are going to feel good."

As he spoke he began pushing the needle in. It was cold then burning hot. I heard him telling me how he was going to fuck me as I felt the metal piercing through my tender flesh, the endorphins from the pain flushing my face and making me woozy. It was almost orgasmic. And it was in.

“There, that wasn’t that bad.” He stood up and surveyed his handiwork, slipping out of his boxers and allowing his thick dick to spring fully to attention.

He opened the drawer of his bedside table and brought out another, matching needle. Then he knelt again.

“Are you okay?” he asked me; his eyes were sparkling.

Through my reverie I managed to nod. He smiled, white teeth shining. He came toward me, bringing his mouth down over the untouched breast. I felt his tongue caressing the brown skin made smooth by excitement. My other tit was straining itself against the metal lodged inside, increasing my pain and arousal to a point where I was again dangerously close to climax. He removed his warm mouth and I felt the cold air, then, slowly, so slowly, he began pushing the other needle. The pain made me high and his voice hypnotized me. He was agonizingly slow and I imagined with what tenderness he would glide his huge cock into my wanting cunt.

The second needle was through.

He slid his hand over his long dick. “Beautiful,” he whispered. I had stopped breathing long ago.

From the bedside table came two matching heavy silver rings. He held them up for me to see.

“Do you like them?” he asked, “I went to three different shops to find these. They’re perfect for you.”

I nodded, wondering how my old bras would rub against that heavy silver, afraid they would look so obvious against a white T-shirt, excited at the thought of him gently tugging them as he pulled me close.

He slid the needle out quickly. The sharp pain was replaced with a rush that forced me to cry out from the intensity. He pushed the pointed spike of the earring through and hooked the loop. I moaned. My nipple was dragged downwards by the ring’s heaviness. The pain faded into a dull ache. He did the other one with the same quick yet precise care. My entire body seemed to hang forward with the weight of the metal. He lifted my chin. Now even his touch was electric. I was overly sensitized, ready to come in an instant. His tongue was so warm in my mouth, his hands so firm as they undid the buckles.

My head was spinning as he lifted me and laid me back on the bed. Every nerve ending of my body led directly to the metal hoops. I was a magnet waiting for a charge.

"You are so beautiful," he said, and reached down and pulled on one of the hoops. I cried out in that fine mixture of pain and pleasure. He smiled. He began to lick inside the silver circle, at the same time opening my hot pussy with his cock. He picked up a ring with his teeth as he entered me. I no longer knew where I was. My body was flooded with the most acute sensations I had ever experienced. I thrust my hips to meet him as he plunged in deeper, his tongue finding the sore bud beneath the silver. With his mouth on one breast he lifted his hand and began rubbing the other nipple with his fingers. All of my blood followed his fingers.

I yelled as he moved into me, fucking me hard and fast. My entire body was on edge and I had never hurt so bad, yet felt so good. As he plunged once more I began to come, but this was different. This didn't begin in my stomach and burn through me, this orgasm was centered around those two metal rings, just like a perfect, silver, O.

Bad Girls in Bondage

Thomas S. Roche

Merrill knew she really should have asked first before she borrowed the ball gag. Sneaking into your roommates' room to use their sex gear without asking was quite inconsiderate. But it's not like she planned the thing. It just sort of... happened, and once things got going it was kind of hard to stop. And before long, Merrill didn't *want* to stop.

She had discovered that Aaron and Esa were kinky shortly after she moved in. Esa had made it quite clear; she didn't want Merrill to think all those whimpers and slaps coming from their bedroom were signs of domestic abuse. Merrill had been embarrassed; she murmured something about that being cool and let it stand at that. Esa could tell she'd embarrassed her new roommate, and so she just mentioned that if Merrill had any questions she should go ahead and ask them—"I'm not shy."

"Um...no, I don't think I really have any questions," Merrill had said in response, turning several shades of red. But in truth, she really had about a zillion questions—from who tied up whom to how Merrill could do it herself. She'd been fantasizing about bondage a lot ever since then; it had occasionally been one of her favorite fantasies, but now she just couldn't get it out of her mind. She kept meaning to ask Esa for more details, but never got up the nerve. Merrill was fairly shy and it was a little uncomfortable for her to ask about such things—especially as they related to what Esa and Aaron actually did in bed, since Merrill had found her roommates making more than a few guest appearances in her fantasies.

Who *did* tie up whom, Merrill often wondered. She usually heard Esa yelping in response to slaps and swishes, but other times she heard nothing more than muffled groans, so maybe they switched. Merrill liked the idea of Aaron trussed up on the bed as Esa spanked him, but she liked even more the idea of Esa being tied spread-eagled as Aaron gave her a good spanking, warming her caramel-colored buttocks, and then entering her from behind, fucking Esa as she pushed her elegant ass up into the air, shoving herself onto him.

That image never failed to make Merrill come.

Esa was truly gorgeous, one of those beauties that porn writers liked to describe as "exotic" and that multiculturalists probably had some other, more politically correct term for. She was fourth-generation Japanese American (what the hell was that, anyway, Quansei or something?) and sixth-generation Italian American, her flawless skin a lustrous mix of olive and café-au-lait, her lips full, the contour of her nose offering just a hint of Rome.

Esa was smart as a whip, in her third year of a Doctorate in Linguistics, and had the kind of confidence that always caused Merrill to melt. Merrill recognized quite clearly that she had a hopeless crush on her roommate, but that, like most of her crushes on women, it was essentially harmless. But that didn't prevent Esa from showing up in Merrill's most torrid fantasies, whether she was the one doing the spanking of Merrill's creamy-white bum or whether she was using her slim fingers to guide Aaron's cock between Merrill's recently-reddened buttocks.

Nothing would come of it, of course. Merrill would never have dreamed of having her first tryst with a woman who also happened to be her roommate—she had seen enough of that in the dorms to know what kind of havoc it would wreak on the domestic situation. But she thought about it an awful lot.

Which is maybe how it started, that night Esa and Aaron went to an eight o'clock jazz concert.

Merrill figured they'd be out until at least midnight, so she was looking forward to a long evening alone. She liked to walk around the house nude; it gave her a strange feeling of entitlement, even freedom. It kind of turned her on. And since Merrill's very favorite thing to do when she had the house to herself was to wank in the living room, she savored that arousal as it built through the evening.

Looking at the video wasn't really a bad thing. When Merrill moved in, Esa told her she could watch any of their videotapes, listen to any of their music. Esa and Aaron being that sort of people, their porn videos sat right out on the living room shelf with everything else. There were only a couple of them, really: *Bad Girls in Bondage*, *Spank Me!*, *Dangerous Lovin'*. Merrill settled upon *Bad Girls in Bondage* and relaxed into the leather sofa with her vibrator.

The video was a bit embarrassing—it wasn't so much the subject matter as the production values: plastic surgery and bad lighting. Purely lesbian action, something that rather disappointed Merrill. She hadn't seen much porn, but she'd long ago decided that as much as she liked women, were she to watch porn videos she would rather see the ones with really big dicks—as big as possible, preferably.

Merrill watched the big-haired lesbians flogging each other and saying things like "Yeah, you love it, don't you, bitch?" It was pretty cheesy. Still, there was something especially hot about watching it in the living room. Merrill had gotten so turned on anticipating her evening alone that she was wet before she started. She was really close to coming before the first spank ever landed on a meticulously liposuctioned ass. But she savored it. She tried to get into the video and found before too long that she was succeeding. When the dominatrix brought out the ball gag and forced it into her victim's mouth amid squeals and whimpers, Merrill felt a surge of arousal. She always got turned on by the idea of being gagged.

Which is when it hit her, so maybe she could blame it on the porn video.

Maybe Esa and Aaron have a gag, Merrill thought.

She knew she shouldn't go in there without asking, and she certainly shouldn't borrow their bondage gear. But Merrill was so turned on that she wasn't thinking straight, and it seemed like a really good idea. After all, it was only ten, and her roommates wouldn't be home for at least two hours. She could borrow some stuff and put it back again without them knowing.

Feeling decidedly naughty and somewhat guilty, she tiptoed into her roommates' bedroom and looked around. There were leather restraints attached to each corner of the neatly-made bed, a riding crop resting on the pillow. Merrill felt a surge of excitement go through her naked body, and knew she was doomed. She was going to do it, even though she shouldn't.

She found their bondage cache on the first guess. She opened the drawer of the nightstand and felt her breath catching in her chest as she looked at an impressive array of ropes, shackles and gags. Merrill could feel her pussy throbbing as she picked through the drawer, caressing each item and fantasizing about Aaron using it on Esa—or using it on *her*.

She selected a pair of matte black handcuffs, making sure to take the key. She couldn't resist taking the ball gag, too—it seemed a little big for her, but the idea of being gagged was such a turn-on for her that she couldn't resist.

Then she spotted the collar. It was a simple one, plain black leather, thick, clearly intended to be a dog collar. It buckled and had a heavy D-ring that you could attach a leash to.

Wow, thought Merrill. *I wonder who wears that.*

Before she knew it, she'd slipped the collar around her throat and buckled it. She felt an intense warming inside her as she ran her fingertips over it, feeling the place where the rough leather touched her smooth neck. The collar gave an added edge of submission to Merrill's fantasy, and she could feel herself getting still wetter, her nipples hardening as she took the handcuffs, key, and ball gag into the living room.

Relaxing into the couch as *Bad Girls in Bondage* continued playing on the screen, she opened her mouth and inserted the ball gag. It certainly was very big, a little hard for Merrill to get her lips around. She strapped it around her head and buckled it, overwhelmed with arousal as she tried to make a noise and got only a strangled yap. She was helpless. Helpless.

She put her wrists behind her back and clicked the handcuffs closed. Moaning into the ball gag, Merrill squirmed on the couch, fantasizing that she was in the video (only without the big hair and bad lighting). Maybe Esa and Aaron were the stars. Merrill was handcuffed, and her two roommates were working her over. She was on her knees with her head in Esa's lap, smelling her roommate's pussy. Aaron was behind them, spanking Merrill. Then, when the moment came, Aaron forced Merrill's legs open and entered her from behind, fucking her as Esa cradled Merrill's face and pushed her head back to kiss her ball-gagged mouth.

Merrill pushed her thighs together tightly, wishing she could reach her vibrator and get it between her legs. She forced her thighs together rhythmically, feeling her pleasure mount, amazed that it almost felt like she could come just from doing that. She was very, very close.

Which is when she heard the footsteps at the bottom of the stairs.

She looked at the clock: 10:45.

No. They couldn't be home early. They just couldn't.

Merrill had tossed the key casually on the sofa next to her. She squirmed over, grabbed it, and fitted the key into the lock of the handcuffs. She had to get everything back into the nightstand before her roommates made it up the stairs.

She turned the key.

Nothing happened.

Merrill started to panic. The key didn't even fit right; it was much too loose in the lock. She'd gotten the wrong key.

Forgetting about the porn video, Merrill leapt up from the couch and ran, still ball-gagged, collared and handcuffed, into the bedroom. She pushed up against the nightstand and worked the drawer open with her cuffed hands. She reached in and began to fish around, but couldn't find any keys.

She went to turn around so she could look through the drawer—maybe she could move stuff around with her nose or something, find the key, then turn around and get it with her hand.

But she lost her balance as she turned. She went down, ass in the air, onto the bed.

Oh, fuck, she thought as she heard the key in the lock.

Esa and Aaron were talking jovially about the concert and how great it was that even though the opening act had canceled, the headliner had played a few extra minutes. And it was so nice to be home early.

"Hey, is Merrill home?" she heard Aaron asking.

"Looks like she's been watching our porn, that naughty girl," said Esa playfully. "This is one of my favorites."

Merrill heard the familiar dropping of keys and opening of closet doors that signified a couple coming home. She lay there, helpless, on her belly, cuffed and nude. This was going to be really, really embarrassing.

She looked up from the bed to see Esa standing there, dressed divinely in a short leather skirt, black stockings, high heels and a black top.

"My, my," she said. "You *are* a naughty girl. Merrill, I had no idea."

Merrill tried to make a noise, but the ball gag had effectively silenced her. She looked at Esa with pleading eyes, hoping her roommate would just find the handcuff key and not embarrass her too much.

Instead, she called to her boyfriend. "Aaron," she said. "Come look at this! It looks like Merrill wants to play."

Aaron appeared in the doorway, his eyes wide. A smile broke across his face as Esa sauntered toward the bed, her hips swaying. Her smile was sexy, evil and gorgeous. Merrill felt heat pulsing through her cunt as Esa sat down on the bed next to her and ran her hand up the back of Merrill's naked thigh. Esa's hand grasped Merrill's medium-length blonde hair and tugged, giving her the sense of Esa's authority, and her own helplessness.

"Is that true, Merrill?" she cooed. "Do you want to play?"

Merrill instinctively tried to shake her head, but found herself all but paralyzed. The pull of Esa's strong hand in her hair had absolutely melted her. The embarrassment didn't help, and it occurred to Merrill that what was happening, ultimately, wasn't embarrassing at all. Not as much as what *could* have been happening.

So she nodded, her eyes wide, looking up helplessly at her roommate.

Esa's hand slipped between Merrill's thighs and Merrill squirmed as she felt those slender, elegant fingers stroking between her swollen pussy lips. Pleasure flooded through Merrill's naked body as she felt Esa tugging firmly on her hair.

"My, my," said Esa. "She definitely wants to play. She can hardly wait. She's dripping. Come feel this, Aaron."

Merrill shut her eyes tight as Aaron pressed his fingers between her legs, feeling how wet she was. He uttered a noise of approval and slid two fingers easily into her. Merrill almost came. She felt herself pushing back against Aaron, coaxing his fingers deeper into her. Esa reached under and started playing with Merrill's clit. The whole room began to spin, and Merrill whimpered helplessly behind the gag. She could smell the mingled scents of Esa's body oil and her sweat, and deep underneath the faintest hint of sex. Esa stood up while Aaron explored Merrill more deeply with his fingers. Esa unzipped her skirt, let it fall, stepped out of it.

She wasn't wearing any underwear. There was only a black lace garter belt hitched to the lace tops of her stockings. Merrill couldn't believe how gorgeous she looked, her long, slender legs framed by black lace.

"Let's give this naughty girl a spanking," said Esa. She climbed onto the bed and Aaron helped her position Merrill's body so that her face was in Esa's lap. Now she *could* smell sex, right against her face, the close-trimmed brush of Esa's pubic hair teasing her lips where they parted wide around the ball gag. The scent turned Merrill on even more, and as Aaron positioned her legs wide apart, she spread them still further. She could feel her nipples, hard and sensitive, rubbing against the bedspread.

Aaron knelt on the edge of the bed and stroked Merrill's pussy some more, coaxing more juices out of her. Then he lifted his hand and brought it down on Merrill's rounded ass. The sting flowed through her, exciting her further. He spanked her rhythmically, softly at first, then more firmly as she began to wriggle and push her ass back toward him, begging for it.

Meanwhile, Esa looked into Merrill's upturned face, her dark eyes seducing her, a faint smile on Esa's full, kissable lips. The scent of Esa's pussy grew stronger; Merrill knew that her roommate was getting wet.

Aaron continued spanking her. Every ten blows or so, he would pause and ease his fingers into Merrill, making her surge with pleasure. Then he would return to the spanking, and the alternation of pleasure and pain brought Merrill almost to the edge of rapturous tears.

When her pale, round ass was so red and hot she couldn't stand it any more, she looked up into Esa's eyes. Esa smiled.

"She's been such a good girl," Esa cooed. "She deserves some sort of reward, doesn't she?"

"Without a doubt," said Aaron.

"From the way she's squirming, I think she needs to get fucked. Is that right, Merrill? Do you need to get fucked?"

Merrill felt herself nodding, without the slightest hesitation.

"Do you want Aaron to fuck you?"

She nodded.

She shut her eyes tight as Aaron took his clothes off. "Open your eyes," said Esa. "I want to look into your eyes as he enters you."

Merrill obeyed, looking up helplessly into her roommate's eyes. She felt the weight of Aaron mounting the bed. He reached under her hips to lift her up onto her knees, so her ass was upturned and her spread legs exposed her waiting pussy. Merrill felt the head of his cock teasing its way between her lips.

Her eyes went wide, held firmly by Esa's, as Aaron entered her. She came almost immediately, his quick thrusts bringing her over the edge so that she bit down onto the ball gag and almost dislodged it. Her whole naked body shook as she came, and Aaron fucked her faster.

"Such a pretty mouth," said Esa, reaching for the buckle of the gag. "It's a shame to gag it."

Esa unbuckled the gag and before Merrill knew what she was doing, she'd buried her face between Esa's spread thighs and was hungrily eating her pussy. The taste was sharp, inviting, exciting Merrill still more. Esa moaned loudly as Merrill licked from her pussy to her clit and back again, then settled on Esa's clit and began to tongue it rhythmically. Aaron fucked Merrill faster and as the taste of Esa's cunt stimulated her still more, she realized she was going to come again. Esa was faster, though, and as Merrill focused on Esa's clit she grasped Merrill's hair and pulled her face tighter between her thighs, begging: "Don't stop...don't stop!"

Esa came just before Merrill did, and her cries were lost in the twist and shudder of Merrill's naked body as Aaron pounded into her. Aaron's climax followed only a moment later, and Merrill pushed back hard onto him, milking his cock as she felt it fill her. Esa ran her fingers through Merrill's hair, smiling down at her.

Moments later, Merrill heard Aaron fishing his keys out of his jeans and felt him unlocking the handcuffs. Her hands came away and Esa began to massage her tingling wrists, getting circulation back into them.

"Such a naughty girl," said Esa. "Such a bad girl, planning this whole thing and springing it on her unsuspecting roommates. Aren't you a bad girl, Merrill?"

Merrill sighed. All things considered, it would be too much work to explain the whole thing—and what would be the point?

So: "Yes," she said. "I'm a very, very bad girl."

"Just the way we like you," said Esa, and Aaron hastened to agree.

Blushing Beauty

Emilie Paris

When you look at me with those stern eyes, I forget how to speak. Every thought evaporates from my mind, and I magically transform back into some high school teenybopper, coming face-to-face with her number one crush. My heart pounds so timpani-loud that I'm sure you can hear it as well. My breathing catches in my throat, and when I exhale, I do so in a desperately shuddering rush. Although I try my best not to blush, somehow I can't help it. Fierce flames lick at my skin from the inside, and my cheeks turn their normal pre-punished shade of deep cherry.

It's the change in you that creates the change in me. Usually, you're so deeply sensitive to my every need that I could ask for nothing more from a lover. You brew me my French Roast coffee in the morning so that I can smell that hearty aroma even before I get out of bed. You surprise me with my favorite flowers on a midweek evening for no reason at all except that you saw the bouquet in the florist's window and the colorful blooms made you think of me.

And all of that is good and fine and straight out of a Hallmark card—but when you get that other look in your eyes, that dark and somber look, I know that I'm in for something serious. Something that will most likely involve my naked form bound in the center of the bed, finely-boned wrists captured firmly over my head in regulation steel cuffs, slim ankles spread wide apart on our jade-green satin sheets.

"You know what I want," you say to me, and I feel your fingertips under my chin, tilting my head upwards so that my eyes will meet yours. But I am defiant this evening, and I close my eyes tightly even as I tremble in your embrace.

What makes me disobey? I don't know. The willful part, I suppose. The part of me that craves punishment to the extreme. The part that wants you to make me behave. *Make me*, I think. *Just make me.*

"Look at me, baby," you say, and I swallow hard and try to pull out of your grip, but that only wins me a laugh from you. Not your normal laugh, but darker, more sinister sounding. "Now," you insist, holding me tighter still.

One segment of my personality truly *does* want to be good for you. One half wishes I could obey and do exactly what you request. But the other part, the bad part, is stronger, and it takes you slapping my cheek to make me obey. "That's right," you continue when I open my eyes in response to the stinging blow. "I want you to watch me very carefully."

So I do. I watch as you slowly take your belt out of your slacks. Your movements seem almost choreographed. I suck in my breath as I watch you pull on the buckle so that the oily length of leather slips gently free from the loops. That belt on the move makes me wetter still. How can a belt turn me on? A belt slipping free, that is. A belt on its way to some use other than holding up a pair of slacks.

For an instant, everything seems too much for me. I want to flee so that you'll have to chase me down the hall, pin me down on the floor and then carry me back to the bed. My stomach tightens, and I taste metal in my mouth. I think about times in the past when I've been disobedient, pulling out of your grip and streaking through the house. You've caught me in the living room, where you bent me over the sofa and spanked me hard with your bare hand. You've caught me in the bathroom, where you cuffed my wrists to the stainless steel towel bar, lubed me up, and fucked my ass. And you've caught me before I could even exit the room, throwing me over your shoulder and dumping me back onto the bed.

Tonight, with X-rated visions in my head, I manage to stay still. Instead of running, or hiding, or begging, I bite on my bottom lip and stare as you double the belt and snap it violently in the air. No sound has ever been so loud, so echoing in my head.

"Bend over," you say. "Bend over and hold on to your ankles."

I move immediately, shivering slightly as I feel the air rustle against my skin. The edge of your belt runs over my ass. Just touches it in a little, leathery stroke. I know what it will be like when you land the first blow, and I wait for the hot fire of it to land against my skin. My heart is pounding forcefully again, my mind on hold. You let the belt smack lightly against my ass. The leather is heavy and makes a solid sound when it connects. But there's no force behind the blows. Not yet. You're in the warm-up stages. Like swinging a bat to get the feel before stepping up to the plate.

Excitement wells within me, and I try to imagine what the pain will feel like when you let the belt land. But then suddenly you change your mind and make my initial fantasy of the evening come true after all. Lifting me in your arms, you carry me to the bed, catch my wrists and cuff them over my head, spread my legs and bind my ankles. I turn my face against the smooth plane of the sheets and wait for the first blow to land. It will hurt, I know. It always hurts. It has to hurt.

You take your time. Silently, you admire the way I look, naked and bound for your enjoyment, and you run your hand over my ass and then cup my cheeks gently. I feel the wetness between my legs already starting to coat my pussy lips, and I sigh and try hard not to grind my hips against the mattress. I know the way you want me to act. Impatience never wins me any points with you. If I want to impress you, then I need to behave. To become one with the pain. To submit and take what you have to give.

After a moment, you snap the belt again, and I jump—or I would, if I had any slack. Instead, I tense. My whole body becomes tight and at the ready, and I feel like a captured animal, one who has been stunned into silent confusion and momentary obedience. You keep waiting until I finally settle into the bed again, as close to relaxing as I can possibly get in this awkward position, and it is then that you land the first stroke.

That blow is a wake-up call—an erotic reminder of what a thrashing with your belt really feels like. Sure, I think about this all the time. It's my number one masturbatory fantasy, as I'm certain you know. Late at night, my fingers work their magic over my clit, stroking and strumming me onward to solo climaxes. The bed shudders with my personal pleasure, as I do my best not to wake you. But when I'm not actually in the moment of being punished, I can't remember what a whipping actually feels like. The image is blocked from my awareness, or locked away somewhere in the recesses of my head. I can't remember what pain is—I only know that it makes me come.

Only when you're in the act of disciplining me, *then* do I know. I know each time the belt lands on my skin, with its spark of instant pain and the aftershocks of sweeter, softer pain that follow. My body remembers and absorbs the intense power of your strikes. Every sensation is magnified within me, concentrated at my very core. By this I mean that my pussy is overflowing now. Because pain turns me on. Receiving it, that is.

This is just a little pain, too. I know the real stuff even if it's rare for you to deal it out. We save the pure dark levels of true lasting pain for special times. But deep down inside I am the total masochist to your ferocious sadist, and I know how to take what you have to give. Tonight, however, you're teasing me. Turning me on in a way that is gentle by your definition. Nothing more than a rhythmic belting on my naked hide. A slap-slap-slapping of the leather on my skin. But it's enough to get my sweet satiny juices running, and when you climb behind me on the mattress, undoing my ankles so that you can slide your cock in easily underneath me, I sigh harshly with untold relief.

Take me, I want to beg. *Work me*, I want to scream. Yet I stay self-contained, waiting, knowing that if I can hold myself together, you will fulfill each one of my most filthy fantasies. I don't need to spell them out for you. That's what makes us so good together. Why would I have to tell you something that's true for you as well? True in reverse, anyway. I want you to spank my bare ass until I can feel the heat radiating through my whole body. That's what makes me wet. *You* want to spank my ass for me until you can admire the purple heat on my once pale skin. That's what makes you hard.

Now, as you fuck me, your strong hands can't stop playing with the welts. Your fingers press on the stripes driven into my skin. I can visualize what the marks must look like, that deep berry hue etched into my supple ass. Your hands dig in, but I hardly feel them. All I know now is the pleasure of your cock. How big it feels inside me. How hard you drive forward with each thrust. Your open hand catches against my ripe, round ass, and you spank me in the exact rhythm that you fuck me. I bounce on the mattress with each blow, and my pussy contracts hard. I love the way that feels. The blissful thrill of pain reconnecting with my most base form of pleasure. I can't come without a combination of the two, and you know that. Oh, how well you know that.

"Good girl," you say. "You squeeze me." You're not issuing a command, you're making a statement. Because each time your hand meets my ass, I contract on you hard. I can't help it. The sensation makes me clench down. It's an automatic response, but it's one that you appreciate. You spank me until I can't remember the feeling of owning an unpunished ass. I am hot and throbbing all over and that has turned my pussy into a lake of sticky sex juices. If I ever doubted how much I need what you have to give me, this is the refuting testimony. My body proves how well we are suited for one another. I arch my back and gaze into space as I come, seeing nothing and everything in a red-hazed blur. I'm glowing. I can feel it.

You come a moment after me, pushing me further until those waves take me away again. Once and then twice, and then three times, until I can't fathom that anything could ever feel better.

"Beauty," you say when you uncuff my wrists and hold me in your arms, "Such a blushing beauty."

A Betting Man

Sage Vivant

"Allen! Come out here and look at this!" Kay called back to him from outside on the terrace of their hotel room.

"Be right there," he responded distractedly. He was checking his pockets for the seventeenth time since leaving New Jersey, confirming that the travelers' checks were all present and accounted for.

He opened the navy vinyl wallet from American Express and rifled through the enormous stack of blue-and-white notes. Forty-four grand, just as he'd placed it there yesterday. Better check that the duplicate receipts were in the suitcase. He'd seen an exposé on "60 Minutes" once that showed how baggage handlers ransacked luggage—

"Allen!"

He clucked his tongue softly, irritated. He'd have to check the suitcase in a minute, after he'd appeased Kay.

"What is it?" he asked, barely hiding his impatience. But as he stepped out the French doors, the view answered his question. The twelve-foot-wide terrace stretched nearly thirty feet forward, bigger than many hotel rooms he'd known. A marvel of craftsmanship and design with mosaic tiles and wrought-iron railings, the terrace was merely the means of revealing the serene Port of Monaco lying beneath them in glittering splendor, with the Alps-Maritimes foothills backing that famous narrow ribbon of coastline. The view astonished them both into silence.

Kay turned to watch him succumb to the majestic scene. Smiling, she said, "See? Aren't you glad I dragged you out here?"

He walked around behind her and pulled her into his arms. "It's breathtaking," he agreed. "Much prettier than the room."

Their room was indeed a disappointment. They'd read extensively about Monte Carlo's hotels and ultimately decided on the Hotel de Paris, expecting unsurpassed elegance. What they received was a room that looked a hell of a lot like something out of a pre-renovation Hilton in the American Midwest.

Neither of them cared, though. There was so much else to be excited about—who minded if the furniture was tacky and the molding dirty?

"Look! There's the palace!" Kay whispered reverently, pointing. Allen saw the palace, but only briefly. He'd fixated on *Le Casino*.

"I'm going to unpack," he said, heading back inside to take inventory of those duplicate receipts.

A few short weeks earlier, their trip to Las Vegas had begun as a lark, an excursion to the greatest man-made showplace on earth. When Kay won $50,000 at the Roulette table, they hightailed it back to New Jersey with a million theories about what to do with their winnings. Buy a house or a car, play the stocks, divvy up the loot among needy relatives?

"Rich people leverage it," Allen had said.

"Rich people don't win their fortunes in one lucky Las Vegas fling. People who win money aren't known for holding on to it," Kay warned.

"I think we're on a lucky streak."

"Allen..."

"How does Monte Carlo sound? Say, next month, after Max's play closes?"

Her hesitation translated into a trip to Monaco.

Kay now followed him into the suite and caught him counting the travelers' checks. She draped herself like an expensive suit across his valise on the bed.

"Your money is just fine, baby. But your wife craves a little attention," she taunted sweetly.

He grinned but kept counting. "Honey, just let me get organized here."

"Has it come to this, then?" she pined, melodramatically. "Even in the face of such seductive beauty, your money has more appeal than my dripping wet pussy?"

He slipped a hand beneath her skirt till he reached her warm, silk-covered mound. "Of course not," he assured her as he stroked her through the panties. "But I want to get this money locked up right away. We want to be able to leverage tonight, don't we?"

"I had hoped to leverage body parts, not cash," she purred, rotating her hips under his fingers.

"Hold that thought. I need to take care of this *other* wad first." And he was out the door.

Two hours later, he returned breathless and glowing. He found Kay on the terrace with a tray of assorted cheeses and a bottle of Merlot. She didn't turn to greet him, but sipped from her wineglass as he approached.

"Kay! I just won four thousand francs!"

"Really." Her voice was cold and she stared at the horizon.

"That's about a thousand dollars!" he continued, enthusiastically.

"I suppose it is." She looked at him now. "What made you come back here?"

With a flourish, he poured himself a glass of wine.

"To tell my favorite woman about it, of course!" he declared expansively, trying to touch his glass to hers. She pulled away.

"What's wrong?" he asked, suddenly aware that it shouldn't have taken him this long to notice her glacial demeanor.

"I feel like you could be here without me and it wouldn't matter. You're completely obsessed with winning. We're in Monte Carlo for excitement, not just for gambling."

He stood before her and bent to kiss her forehead. He was more than willing to admit he was acting like a jerk, especially if an admission was what it took to restore her characteristic cheerfulness.

"I'm sorry," he said after he pressed his lips to her brow. "I'll make it up to you."

"How?"

"Dinner at Louis XV?"

"We *have* to eat. That's nothing special."

"Some jewelry? There's a store on every corner. Diamonds everywhere!"

"No." She placed her empty glass on the small table and leaned back in her chaise. "You need to remember what makes us alive. And it's not money."

His pulse quickened and an unnamed current worked its way through his body. "I think you've got a plan."

"Walk this way," she commanded, leading him into the suite.

Once inside, she ordered him to remove his pants. He complied, grinning at the sound the slacks made as they whooshed down to his feet.

"Give me your ass," she whispered, pushing him gently onto the bed. He got on all fours and she knelt on the floor so her face was level with his smooth, waiting buttocks. She spread his cheeks and ran her tongue in a wet line between them. He moaned. She focused more attention on his puckered little hole. With each lap of her tongue, his muscle relaxed a bit more.

After some expert rimming, she forced him to beg for tongue-fucking. "Tell me what you want," she insisted.

"Please, Kay—"

But instead of her agile tongue, a harder, larger item pushed a slick path into him. He tried to look behind him but couldn't discern what she was doing. When he felt the flat wings of the item against his cleavage, he knew a butt plug was firmly ensconced.

She twisted it gently and spoke to him in level tones. "We'll have a lovely dinner at Louis XV and then we'll hit the casino. And you will not remove the toy until I say you can."

She didn't speak with cruelty or malice. How well she knew that, for him, wearing a butt plug as he moved about the world was a delectable prospect. They often talked of it but he never dreamed she'd make him wear one. He got to his feet as she unwrapped a line of flesh-colored duct tape from a sizable roll.

"Don't tell me the hotel supplied that," he said, wide-eyed.

"Eh, the French," she winked as she wrapped a thick ribbon of tape around his pelvis, making sure to cover the end of the butt plug to anchor it. "Nothing fazes them."

She cut the end and got to her feet. "You're strapped in for the night, sweetheart," she announced, checking him over like he was a repair job she'd just completed. "But we'll need to test my handiwork before we send you out. Think of it as quality control."

She sauntered over to her suitcase and extracted the handcuffs he recognized from home. A surge of gratitude and sentiment swept through him but she left him little time to dwell on it.

"Follow me," she said over her shoulder as she headed for the terrace.

Their bondage play had always been confined to the bedroom back in New Jersey. This Monaco lifestyle had already started to go to her head, he observed silently. Nevertheless, he scurried behind her.

"Have a seat," she instructed, dangling the cuffs so they sparkled in the moonlight. She nodded towards one of the cushioned wrought-iron chairs. At first, he stood, mute and outrageously hard, astonished by her boldness as well as his nakedness. He glanced around furtively to satisfy himself that no other guests saw him bottomless on the terrace, then lowered himself into the seat.

She cuffed him quickly, clicking away at his wrists, her efficiency just making him harder. The butt plug wedged its way deeper up his chute but he fought against showing her the pain on his face because it would have prompted her to adjust the plug somehow and he liked it exactly where it was.

She whipped her full skirt up and sideways to reveal her *sans panties* fashion statement. "Now then, let the testing begin," she said quietly, with a leg on either side of the chair and her wet pussy slowly devouring his rock-hardness. Between the cuffs and the weight of her body, he was immobilized. Every sensation, every thought now emanated from his genitals in throbbing, electrified pulses. He was vaguely aware of wanting to touch her, but forced himself to let his cock do the touching, caressing the inside of her in juicy strokes while the cheering section in his ass pounded its applause.

He could no longer control the expression on his face. As she rode him, harder and faster, the cuffs clanged against the iron detailing of the chair. He should have been more conscious of the kind of spectacle they were likely to be presenting, either now or soon, but all his brain could handle was the intense heat between his legs and how glorious it was to surrender to Kay's thorough quality control methods.

That evening, she wore a dress he'd never seen before. Deep emerald-green panné velvet draped and clung to her form with sublime perfection. Kay's was a body that defined voluptuousness: round, shapely, strong. Often Allen would look at her and think only of being engulfed in her abundant sensuality. She glowed with femininity—not by modern-day emaciation standards but in classic goddess style.

Tonight, she was particularly radiant. They dined on the lighter side of Chef Ducasse's "Pour Les Gourmets" menu, for this evening they could not risk being sluggish. Before the appetizer, Kay traced her finger along the swell of her breasts and asked if he wouldn't like to have his cock between her tits. After the entrée was served, she let him know that she hadn't forgotten about their little secret.

"If my tongue was in there, I'd have you squirming for the wait staff," she whispered during dessert, her eyes sparkling.

The plug's presence induced an unwavering alertness he knew he could not sustain indefinitely. Allen sat across from his wife with a hard-on that trembled with confusion. He was ready to go back to the hotel immediately, but Kay had other plans.

"Shall we gamble?" Kay asked after dinner.

It was a short but excruciating walk to the casino. The heavy tape around his hips was uncomfortable but its existence was entirely overshadowed by the stubby toy up his ass. His wife clung to his arm like a countess, her words belying her regal deportment.

"When you walk, does it feel like my finger is wiggling in your hole?"

Instead of answering her directly, Allen paused before ascending the grand steps to the casino.

"Kay, how long do I have to wear this?"

She paused before answering, looking toward the stars as if a set of cue cards were somewhere in the heavens.

"I don't know," she said, finally. "Until this gambling obsession leaves you, I suppose."

"How will I know when that is? How will *you* know it?" Was he alarmed or aroused? He couldn't determine.

"One of us will know when the time is right," she said confidently, pressing her soft, ample body into him. "It'll probably be me," she added.

They entered the casino.

Minutes passed before either of them found words. The old-world opulence of the most famous gambling hall in the world could only be diminished by commentary. Sleek marble frescoes frosted with gleaming gold surrounded them, interrupted by occasional sculptures. Too lush to be a museum, too stately to house such a dubious form of entertainment.

"Which salon, *monsieur*?" asked the graciously officious but clearly chauvinistic maitre d' as he bowed ever so slightly toward Allen, while managing to appear completely unaware of Kay's voluptuous presence.

Allen had his heart set on the *Salons Privés*, where only 11 players at a time were admitted, each of whom had a purse of at least $5,000. He tried to read Kay's expression. Was there an answer to the man's question that might please her? The delicious impalement struggled in vain for mastery over his hunger to win.

"*Salons Privés, s'il vous plaît.*"

They were instantly escorted to the private rooms behind the *Salon Ordinaire* (or "American Room, " as it was commonly known). Kay muttered under her breath.

"You must really enjoy getting fucked."

He wasn't sure if she referred to his salon choice or his well-filled ass.

Kay declined to watch him tango with the high rollers. He gave her some money and she departed for the American

Room, but not before she hissed a warning about not disturbing the tape. He almost said, "What tape?"

In an hour, he'd lost $6,000 at Punto Banco, a game whose rules he hadn't committed to memory. His butt plug stretched him and reverberated when he spoke or moved. The feeling should have been unpleasant but it wasn't, though he knew it marred his judgment and disturbed his sense of timing. He switched to Roulette, the method by which Kay had acquired their small fortune in Las Vegas.

In an instant, he'd won $3,000. In the next, he'd bet it all and lost it.

Suddenly, he was angry with Kay for compromising him in this way. Wasn't the money he hoped to win for both of them? Why was she punishing him? He excused himself from the *Salons Privés* and attempted to stride authoritatively to the American Room. Now the movement was so painful he managed only a comic hobble to Kay's side.

She was playing Blackjack. Stacks of colored chips were piled by her elbow. The sensations between his asscheeks precluded any arithmetical calculations, so he asked her outright how much she had.

"About twelve thousand," she said, coolly.

"Cash out," he blurted quietly.

Wordlessly, she obeyed. Moments later, they left the marble gambling palace. Net gain: $6,000.

They did not speak on the short walk across the Place du Casino to their hotel. His mind was a muddle of ecstatic conflict. Her face was Madonna-like in its inscrutable tranquility.

Once inside their suite, he started to strip off his clothes. She stopped him.

"Not so fast," she said sternly. Mischief played in her eyes. He realized he was unbearably hard and wondered how noticeable this might have been to others all evening. She pushed him gently into an overstuffed chair.

"Take out your cock for me."

She sat across from him on the bed. As he exposed his raging hard-on, she unzipped her dress and let the shoulders fall to her elbows. She wore no bra and the dress now bunched provocatively at her nipple line. Her strong legs were crossed and she leaned forward inquisitively.

"Did you enjoy yourself tonight?" she asked, eyeing his thick rod.

He grinned. "Yes." He recalled being angry with her but couldn't summon that feeling now.

"Why did you enjoy yourself?" She let one breast escape from the velvet.

"Because you gave me pleasure."

"Did I? Didn't the toy do the work?" she teased.

"But each time I moved, I thought of you. The plug was more of a messenger."

She smiled broadly and stood. Her dress rushed to the floor, leaving her completely naked. Her soft fullness loomed before him. She leaned over to the night table, where her stockings lay in a careless, wispy pile.

"What a receptive student you are!" she chuckled. "You learned what was necessary *and* you made money!" Her pussy hovered inches from his face.

"You made the money. Just like last time."

"Either way, it's ours." She grabbed a handful of his hair and pulled him toward her body. Her sleekly shaved pussy shone slightly with juice, and he could think only of burying his nose between her folds. In her other hand, she held the stockings.

"Good students have to eat pussy at Miss Kay's School for Wayward Gamblers," she said, pushing her hips forward. When his tongue touched her smooth mons, the plug jumped and shivered and repositioned itself. The walls of his ass screamed for more as much as they screamed for mercy.

Soon, he was on his knees, lapping at her cunt. She made him keep his hands over his head, where she held them at the wrists and tied them together with her stockings.

Her juice flowed and smeared his chin and cheeks. He contorted himself into a position where his pulse was so strong, the plug fucked him with short stabs. As he ate his wife, she swelled under his tongue. Her scent intensified. He licked wildly, desperate for her to come. When she climaxed, Kay groaned with an undertone Allen felt in her pubis. Gradually, her inner labia stopped twitching and she loosened her grip on his hair.

His ass wanted ramming. Did he dare ask for it?

She fell back on the bed. As she looked at the ceiling, she gave him instructions: "Stand up. Straddle my face."

"But my arms..."

"What about them?"

"They hurt."

She sighed and sat up, her breasts swinging heavily with the movement. She untied his wrists and when his hands fell to his sides, she swiftly used one nylon leg to re-bind them behind his back, then gagged him with the other stocking and tied it behind his head with gentle firmness to muffle any sound from his mouth. Once he was bound to her liking, she sat with her back against the headboard. "Fuck my mouth now, you rich bastard."

He approached her, still wearing the tape belt she'd applied before dinner. She peeled the sturdy adhesive from his skin, unwrapping him like a birthday gift. The plug barely moved from its lodging place of several hours until he bent to kiss her. Then a swift, partial ejection shot a new round of sensations through his beleaguered cavity and he yelled with pleasure.

The plug stopped at its widest point, protruding nearly halfway out of his ass. Kay reached around behind him, grasped the base, and gave it a half-twist. He bolted upright.

She took his cock in her mouth and bobbed on it rhythmically. Her wet lips held him as tightly as her hot cunt would have. And as she mouth-fucked him and pushed and pulled the butt plug, he thought of thrusting his cock into her pussy. Or her ass. He thought of the plug inside him, pumping him. He thought of her juices, the way her tits pressed into his thighs.

And he let go with a harsh groan that echoed inside of him. As the waves of pleasure rocked him, she slowly extracted the plug. He paused to experience the utter deflation of his entire being. Some indefinable balance reasserted itself, to his combined relief and disappointment. She untied the stocking around his head before unleashing his hands.

Looking at him in his demolished state, Kay smirked. "Do you suppose this is what they're referring to when they talk about the thrill of gambling?"

"I don't know," Allen sighed as he rubbed his raw wrists. "I'm not much of a betting man, myself."

The First Pinch

Michele Zipp

Chloe was a bad girl—the kind of bad that makes other people uncomfortable, mostly due to her undeniable sexuality. She was petite, with full, rosy lips, and when she spoke with her curt British accent people hung on her every word. It didn't matter what she said, but she did mostly speak about sex. She was kinky and polite. If her erotic conversation made her listeners uncomfortable, she just moved on. She could be as demure as a schoolgirl, but often that turned people on. She knew how to use it. She was the kind of girl that no-good boyfriends refused to let their girlfriends hang out with. I was single, so it wasn't a problem.

I wasn't the opposite of Chloe, but close. With my ice-blue eyes, it was like I was naturally drawn into hers, which were piercing and dark. From the very first moment I met her, waiting on line behind her in a deli where she came up a quarter short, she did something weird to me. It was like electricity. As she searched her jeans pockets for spare change, I reached into my purse without thinking and held out a quarter. She looked at me out of the corner of her eye and half a smirk brightened her face. As she turned toward me and held out her hand, she whispered "Thank you," and I could smell the sweetness of strawberry on her breath. She paid and waited for me outside.

We were neighbors and ran into each other a lot. She pursued our friendship more than I did. I just thought we were too different. She liked loud bars; I preferred quiet evenings at home. She was bold and confident; I was reserved.

One day, Chloe invited me out to see a friend's band play. We made loose plans and I told her that I might see her there. Unwinding after work, I started my usual routine of sitting in front of the television until I fell asleep. I nodded off at around eight o'clock, but woke up at eleven. For some reason, I decided to take Chloe up on her offer. I freshened up, got dressed, and went out.

When I got there, I spotted her immediately. She was wearing these tight black leather pants with a white mesh T-shirt. No bra. This woman had the most incredible breasts I'd ever seen—and probably the whole bar had ever seen. When I walked over to the booth she was sitting in, she looked up at me and brushed the clump of stray hair that had fallen out of her ponytail away from her eye. She took a drag of her cigarette, put it in the ashtray, looked at me with a tentative smile and said, "Sit down."

"Do you want a drink?" I asked while nervously fidgeting through my purse for my wallet. She hesitated, sighed, twisted her big, puckered lips and said, "Stoli Strawberry sounds good."

"I'll be right back."

I was at the bar when the rush of adrenaline almost overcame me. I didn't know what to make of the way she made me feel. I had never been attracted to a woman before. I looked over in Chloe's direction and saw her talking to one of the guys in the band. She laughed and smoke came out of her sultry mouth. She noticed me looking at her and smiled. I got our drinks and walked back over.

"Alyssa, this is Daniel," she said as if she was a magician and had just created him. Daniel was tall and had shaggy, dirty brown hair. His jeans were slung low on his waist and showed off his thin build.

"Hello," Daniel said politely and held out his hand.

"You would have seen his band play if you had been here a half hour earlier," she teased.

"Oh, I'm sorry. I didn't realize you went on so early," I said and took a sip of my vodka and 7 Up.

"A few of us were going to go back to my place for some drinks," Daniel said. "Would you like to come? "

"Let's go," Chloe urged, nodding insistently at me.

In my car, following Daniel, Chloe and I barely said a word to each other. I could see her looking at me and smiling. I kept my eyes on Daniel's bumper. When we got to his house, Chloe put her hand on my knee and said, "Are you OK?"

"Yeah, why?"

"You were so quiet."

I just smiled.

Daniel's place was gorgeous. A thick, red velvet drape extended from the tall ceiling to the floor separating the living room from the bedroom. The velvet was draped back, so a hint of the bed was visible. It was covered in black velvet and on it sat two cats as black as the bed, four tiger eyes gleaming at me. His couch was soft, deep-green plush; I couldn't help but touch everything. Behind the couch was a hallway leading to the kitchen where Chloe and Daniel had disappeared. They were quiet at first and it was just the three of us there.

"Would you like a drink, Alyssa?" Daniel called out.

"Sure. What do you have?"

"Everything," Chloe said with a giggle.

I got up off the couch and went into the kitchen. Chloe was slowly pouring some red wine into Daniel's mouth with one hand and had his hair tangled and pulled back with the other. I stood there for a moment looking at them with my mouth open. She stopped pouring and Daniel swallowed his mouthful. Chloe wiped the drizzle of red from his mouth with the back of her hand and licked it. Daniel leaned toward me to kiss me.

For a moment, I was lost in his lips. I felt like I couldn't move and there was an incredible feeling of nervousness inside me. I just stood there with my hands still beside me as he kissed me. I could feel Chloe's hand pull me closer towards them. My eyes were closed but I could tell she still had her hand wrapped in his hair because of the jerky movements of his head. I could feel Daniel's hand against my hip. He moved it up under my shirt and Chloe's fingernails trailed behind his. Through my lace bra, Daniel was circling my erect nipple, making it even harder. I could feel the blood rush towards my aching pussy and I wanted to scream in delight, but I was still playing with Daniel's tongue in my mouth. Chloe's fingers traced Daniel's, but then she focused on my nipple and pinched it hard. I opened my eyes, slightly in shock, and Chloe's eyes were focused on me. She grabbed the back of my hair and pulled me towards her just-licked lips. They were as soft as I had imagined. Her lip-gloss was sweet and even though Daniel tasted like wine, Chloe was intoxicating.

There was a knock at the door followed by the rest of Daniel's band and some others walking in. I got so nervous, I quickly said good-bye and left. "I'll call you tomorrow," I could hear Chloe saying as I walked out.

The phone rang once and my eyes opened.

Silence.

The phone rang a second time and with that I extended my left arm, grasped the receiver, and brought the phone to my left ear. I was so tired, but I managed to mutter a hello.

"Hi," Chloe said, half out of breath.

I cleared my throat. It was stale from lack of speaking.

"Meet us for breakfast," she demanded but in a soft tone.

"Where?"

"Daniel's."

After agreeing, I extended my left arm to replace the receiver on the hook and I held my hand there a moment. I closed my eyes tight and wondered if I was up for this. But I was so drawn to them. I took a shower, got dressed, and left.

When I pulled into the driveway, Chloe came out and sat on my hood before I even got out of my car. I hesitated, but she looked at me through the windshield and smiled. I could feel the moist grass on my toes through my sandals as I walked around the car and sat down on the hood near Chloe. The car was warm and there was some steam mixing with the morning mist. Daniel appeared and touched my wet toes resting on the bumper with both his hands and moved between my legs. He kissed me soft and slow and held my face. Chloe wrapped her legs around me from behind. Then Daniel stopped suddenly, lifted me off the car, and carried me into the house with Chloe close behind.

He laid me down on his black velvet bed and it was like I was frozen, but hot all over. Chloe crawled in on all fours from the other room. Her devious grin barely held the leash in her mouth. There were two red leather cuffs attached to each end of the chain. I watched Chloe stand up and walk around the room lighting candles. Daniel was straddling me, holding my arms pinned down on the bed. The only sounds I could hear were my own heartbeat and breath. The uncertainty of not knowing what was next was enough to make me wet, but I could also feel Daniel's dick stiffening against my clit.

Chloe walked towards Daniel's steel-posted headboard and wrapped the chain around it. After he lifted my shirt over my head, Daniel licked his way from my fingers up my arm. Just as he bit down on my neck, Chloe fastened the cuff on my right wrist. She knelt down and kissed the inside of my hand and then allowed me to run my fingers through her hair. Impulsively, I closed my fist and wouldn't let her soft strands go. With both hands, Daniel pinched my nipples simultaneously and didn't release. I let out a soft sigh of pain and looked up into his dark eyes with a yearning to be kissed. Even though his hand was no longer holding down my left arm, it remained pinned on the bed. I wanted to be taken.

Daniel licked his way from my chin to my forehead as Chloe secured the other cuff to my left arm and the bedpost. With one motion, her slip dress fell to the floor. Her milky-white skin clashed against her dark areolas and jet-black pubic hair. She wore a black silk scarf around her neck. As Daniel slid down to the end of the bed, Chloe situated herself on top of my face. I could feel the ends of her pubes tickling my lips and I stuck out my tongue in the hope of tasting her, but she would pull up each time I came close.

My pussy was throbbing. Daniel pulled off my pants quickly and teased the bottoms of my feet with what felt like feathers. I was too busy taking in Chloe's scent to be sensitive to the tickling. Then I felt the heat of candle wax dripping on my thighs. I felt it sting and harden. Daniel removed my panties. He massaged his way up towards the aching folds of my cunt and lightly stroked each side, putting pressure on my now hidden clit. Just as he placed a finger inside my dripping cave, Chloe came down on my face. I entered her with my tongue and as I looked up to see if she approved, she threw her head back in delight. Daniel's warm tongue was making hard circles on my clit. The pleasure was intense, and I did the same to Chloe. By now, my hands were aching to touch my captors and the sound of the chain clanging against the steel bed frame provided a soundtrack to our play.

With his strong hands, Daniel pushed my legs as far apart as they could go. Chloe had switched directions and was facing Daniel, her pussy lips—pink and swollen—held my tongue. I could hear a faint buzz as Chloe's delicate fingers circled my ass, wet from my dripping juices. Daniel worked in a thin vibrating plug and as Chloe played with the speeds, he went to work on my pearl. I could barely lick Chloe's pussy with all the intensely delightful distractions happening to my body. But she insisted and thrashed herself up against me again and again. I moaned louder and louder into her pussy and the vibrations of my sounds made her happy. As Chloe put more pressure on the butt plug, Daniel stuck his dick deep inside my hole and filled me. His perfect hand motions on my clit made me come so hard my walls clamped down almost trapping him inside me.

"Good girl," Chloe purred as she lay on the bed beside me lightly scratching my breasts with her fingernails.

My entire being was limp from being rocked so hard. I was in bliss, but I knew Chloe wasn't through just yet. Without words, she nodded to Daniel who pulled out a large, complicated-looking black leather belt from his closet. He handed it to Chloe and loosened the restraint on my leash.

Daniel slid his body underneath mine. His cock was positioned perfectly between my ass cheeks and was hard against my slit. Chloe slipped the belt under our bodies and tied us together as if lacing up a corset, while Daniel cupped my tender tits. She stood up and strapped on a dildo, and stood above us on the bed for a moment showing off her power with the fake flesh in her hand. She bent down and shoved it in my mouth for a moment, then she untied the scarf on her neck and blindfolded me with it. I could feel her walk to the end of the bed and the bounce made Daniel's dick slide up and down on me.

"Your sweet juices are flowing onto my cock," he whispered into my ear.

"Quiet!" Chloe demanded. I felt her hand slightly tap on my opening as she stroked Daniel's dick. He pinched and pulled at my nipples. The heat surged in my cunt as Chloe tapped the end of the strap-on against my engorged pink clit. Daniel's heavy breathing was lifting my small frame up and down and as Chloe entered me with her package. I was bounced back and forth. I couldn't tell if she was still stroking Daniel, but his breathing became labored and quick. I was reaching ecstasy when Chloe yelled, "Are you ready to please me?"

With that Daniel unbound us from each other and slipped out from underneath me. With my hands still bound and the blindfold on, I had no idea what was happening. I felt Chloe's round breasts on mine. Her lips, which tasted of my own pussy, kissed me hard, deep and passionately. With her hands pulling my hair up towards the headboard, I felt Daniel's legs between my own and Chloe's. He was pounding into her hard. His hand was cupping my cunt with pressure on my clit just right, and between Chloe pounding back onto him and him pumping forward into her, the gyrations brought me once again to the verge.

"Oh," she moaned long and hard with her lips still pressed on mine.

She bit down on my bottom lip and we all collapsed on the bed.

I woke hours later covered up in the soft blankets on Daniel's bed. I was no longer tied up or blindfolded and my entire body ached with pleasure.

Daniel was spooning me from behind and Chloe lay beside me with her eyes open, stroking my hair. The blanket rested just under one of her breasts and I reached out and pinched her nipple. She smiled, her lips puckered, and she closed her eyes.

Strictly Business

Mark Williams

"Honey, have you ever been tied up with pantyhose?" Debbie asked demurely.

"No," I lied, thinking to myself, *"at least not yours, anyway."*

"Well then, maybe it's time. Why don't you take mine off, sweetie? But gently."

I did as instructed, tugging her skirt as high as I could and peeling down her off-black stockings carefully. This was a side of Debbie I'd rarely seen before. Usually she was prim, proper, businesslike. In fact, her pantyhose were typically a badge of her conservatism. She wore them to work under tailored suits, on dates, nearly everywhere. She also wore them to bed on nights when she didn't want me to initiate sex play. Even the panties she wore underneath tonight, though black, were not exactly racy.

I was already down to my favorite pair of purple silk boxers. I'd been trying to rev her up after her long day of sales calls, with little success. I'd gotten only her shoes off, and was stroking her calves and thighs when she hit me with her surprise query.

Her tone suddenly hardened. "You remind me of a client of mine who's a real dick. Everything has to be just his way."

"So what are you suggesting?" I asked, watching her wrap the hose around her hands and pull them taut.

"Maybe you need to be taught a lesson. Maybe all men need to be taught a lesson. Turn around, and put your wrists together."

Again, I did as told. I'd never seen her this authoritative outside of work, and my hard-on was raging with anticipation.

She bound my wrists with the confidence and skill of a Girl Scout. In fact, I remembered her telling me she'd been one many years ago. Must've gotten a merit badge or two in knot tying. Tight. Effective. I realized in seconds that my wrists had been firmly secured. My erection somehow felt harder than it ever had before...or maybe I was simply more aware of it. I sat on the edge of the bed, and Debbie turned me slightly to face her again.

"Those are very expensive pantyhose, my dear, so you'll need to reimburse me later. Those knots probably will have to be cut." Now I was just another business expense.

"Whatever you say, Debra," I purred, wishing she'd pay some attention to my throbbing cock.

Instead, she removed a paisley kerchief from the front pocket of her blazer and folded it in half, forming a long triangle. Sitting next to me, she wrapped the accessory tightly around my eyes without warning, and knotted it securely behind my head.

"Close your eyes and keep them closed," she ordered.

"I really don't have much choice, do I?"

"You talk too much." I heard some rustling. She stood up, sat back down.

"Open your mouth, lover." When I did, she pushed something satiny into it. I realized I was most likely being gagged by her panties. I felt almost dizzy with excitement. She rose again, as the weight beside me on the bed vanished. Seconds later, I heard a sticky peeling sound. What was it?

Tape.

"This will insure that you don't spit them out," she informed me. I heard several peeling and cutting noises, and felt her applying piece after piece to my face. Big pieces; I guessed masking or duct. I was obviously now finished talking clearly, and minus my sight, I felt a bit nervous around her for the first time since we'd met at an art gallery two years earlier and struck up a conversation.

"Lie down, honey. Now, roll over onto your belly."

Again, I obeyed instantly. My hard-on had eased a bit while she applied the tape, but after following her directions, my boner stiffened again as I lay on top of it in my boxers. I could move my wrists only as far as the pantyhose gave, which wasn't much.

"Lift up," she commanded, and I felt her hands tugging at the waistband of my boxers. I obeyed, and she peeled them off aggressively. I felt her shift on the bed, presumably moving next to me.

"I've always liked your ass," she said plaintively. She ran her hands along it, pausing near my anus to suggest she might insert a finger. I held myself rigidly. This wasn't like Debbie at all. There was a pause and I felt moisture—her tongue. A gentle exploration, not a probe. All this from a woman who wouldn't let me go down on her until months into our relationship.

I was again losing myself in a blur of sensations. She snapped me out of it with a hard, brisk slap to my ass. "You don't think I tied you up to lick your butt, do you?"

I hummed an indecisive note through my panty gag.

She rose again. I noticed I was sweating. Nothing I could do about it, though. Portions of the tape holding my gag in place already had begun to peel away from my face due to perspiration.

The next thing I felt was cool moisture in my rear hole. I heard a spurting noise and felt more. Followed by her fingers, rubbing the liquid around my anus, then gently *into* it. Then more firmly, forcing a finger, then two, into my ass. I had again stiffened involuntarily, but found myself relaxing with each probing motion she made. She gave an occasional squeeze to my balls, as well. I began to rub against the bed, suddenly needing to come.

Another hard slap from her on my ass. "Don't you dare!"

I did my very best to obey.

"You're getting nice and loose. Just relax, and do as you're told." She worked her fingers in and out, massaging my prostate gently, then roughly. Little Miss Conservative was getting bolder by the minute. I struggled symbolically against my bonds, even though I knew I couldn't escape and certainly didn't want to.

"Don't resist. Give in to the sensation. You're mine to do with as I please."

I mumbled what was supposed to be a "Yes, Debra." It came out something like "Yeth, Dubba."

"Silence!" She spanked my ass hard yet again, and I felt her rise from the bed. I noticed a warm flushing sensation where she'd slapped me. Lubricant was dripping out of me. A bead of sweat rolled down my forehead, underneath my silky blindfold and into the corner of my left eye. I was forced to blink several times to alleviate the salty sting. My cock was rock hard, and my balls were beginning to ache ever so slightly. Yet I was loving every second of my prim and proper Debra showing me who was boss. A side of her I'd always suspected but never seen before.

I heard rustling noises of all sorts in the background, and tried to focus on those sounds to guess what she had in mind for me. I could tell she was opening and closing a drawer or two, but beyond that I couldn't discern much. I was tingling with anticipation. Here was a woman I had to ease along sexually in our early days together. It was four dates before we'd even kissed passionately. Months before she let me fuck her doggie-style. Her sexual inexperience and hesitancy were often frustrating for me, and I felt I had to guide her in many arenas, often showing her exactly what I liked in bed. Sometimes I wondered if she perhaps resented that.

Was this personal revenge on her part, or was she just showing me a few ideas of her own after all this time? Or was she getting some sort of fantasy vengeance on one of her many sexist-jerk clients? I didn't care. My cock was throbbing. I felt my shoulders starting to ache. I was sweating everywhere. I was miserably uncomfortable, yet completely helpless and totally aroused.

She slid beside me yet again. "You know that mint-green teddy of mine, honey? The one that always gets you going? I've got it on for you, baby. And nothing else. You can't see it and you won't see it, but I wanted you to think about me wearing it." She rubbed a portion of the satiny fabric against my bare ass. "See?"

I grunted through my gag, then made a playful lunge with my bound hands, trying to grab the teddy. If possible, my cock got even harder. She had no trouble pulling away from me.

"Roll onto your side, loverboy," she ordered, and again I complied, although with considerable difficulty. I heard a peeling plastic sound, then felt her cool hands on my warm cock. She began to unroll a condom onto my dick, somewhat awkwardly. At times, the elastic bottom snapped against my penis, but I held in my discomfort, not wishing to anger or embarrass her. When she was satisfied with her work, she rolled me back onto my stomach. Then, silence for several minutes.

Eventually I heard what I believed was a vibrator click on. Another little surprise from her. I didn't even know she owned one. Was she going to pleasure herself while watching me struggle? Or...?

"I bought this for myself," she confessed, "but I'm thinking maybe you should break it in for me."

She traced the pulsating vibrator along my buttcheeks for what had to be several minutes. Time and again she moved it along the ridges of my anus. I wanted it in me, and she knew it. But she made me wait. After what seemed an eternity, she tried to ease the buzzing sex toy into my yielding ass and I grunted loudly.

"Relax, baby. Just give in. You know you want this."

She was right—I did. After another attempt, she eased the vibrator into my yielding butthole and I groaned in total surrender. The hard metal cylinder throbbed and pulsed in my ass, filling me. I took a brief moment to contemplate my situation—my wrists bound with pantyhose, my eyes blindfolded, my mouth filled with panties—all thanks to a woman I'd thought was too businesslike and rigid to ever do such things to me. I wanted her more now than I ever thought possible.

After a night of surprises and uncertainty, I finally felt I knew what was coming next—me. My body spasmed violently as hot jism spewed into the condom Debbie had placed on me. I felt myself ejaculate what seemed to be quarts of come. I was an erupting volcano, and my lava was sperm. My whole body felt the release of orgasm, which seemed to last for a minute or two. When I was finally done, I exhaled heavily through my nostrils and emitted a muffled sigh of relief, release, and pleasure through my gag. I soon felt myself becoming very drowsy and wanted only to rest, to sleep.

Debbie brought an end to that with another hard slap to my ass. "Okay, baby, that was good...now let's see how long it takes you to come a second time. And maybe a third."

The vibrator buzzed along merrily in my ass, and I resigned myself to a long evening of surrender and pleasure. Within a few minutes, I felt my sensitive, tender cock beginning to get rock hard again. What Debbie the businesswoman wanted, Debbie usually got.

Restraining Order

Dante Davidson

Duncan buckled his leather belt around her upper arms, capturing them behind her body. Yolanda was sitting up in the bed, her arms fastened and her whole attitude one of waiting. She didn't fear him, didn't belong to him, but she would let him use her like this for the night. It appealed to her, being so well-restrained when her mind was free and flying, wondering what he would do next. She tilted her head back, looking at him, challenging him with her cold, liquid dark eyes.

With a sigh, Duncan spread her thighs wide, using his callused thumbs to part the petal lips of her pussy, watching her face instead of her cunt. He liked the way Yolanda's face seemed to change as he touched her, those dark eyes half-closed, seeming sleepy, or suddenly relaxed. He continued to probe her, continued to play, using his fingertips to feel for her clit, to brush against it and make her move. Her body was amazing, elongating like an animal's as he stroked her, swan neck thrown back, silky raven hair brushing his pillows.

It was almost hypnotic, the way her slender hips rose and fell on the rough Navajo blanket, the sound of her breath as it caught in her throat. Yolanda arched her waist up and spread her thighs even wider, letting him see the treasure of her sex, hidden there at the split of her body.

Duncan was on his knees at the edge of the bed and he pulled her forward, getting in between her thighs, impaling her with his cock. She shuddered as he entered her, and he could feel the wave of it rush through her body, the tight inner muscles contracting on him like currents of fire.

He reached forward with one hand, stroking her cheek, laying two fingers on her bottom lip, pressing them forward and into her warm, wet mouth. She sucked on his fingers while her pussy milked his cock, and he was out of his head from it, spinning, spiraling, but he needed more. He tugged at the buckle on his belt and freed her, then quickly grabbed her wrists, capturing them together in one hand, holding her tightly, pulling her into an upright position on the bed with her hands high above her head, completely in his power.

He worked her like that, sliding in the satisfying slickness between her legs, bucking against her, driving into her with his entire being. He tried to get a response, a verbal acknowledgment from her, but Yolanda was focused inside herself as he fucked her. She took it all in, everything he did, and processed it—the way she processed pain—understanding, contemplating, knowing that her body would be made to come from it well before her mind.

When his cock was coated with her satiny juices, he pulled out, released her wrists, and ordered her to clean him. She obeyed instantly, bending low on the bed to reach for his throbbing member. She took it into her mouth, into the velvet heat of her mouth, lapping at the juices that had dripped to the base of his cock. Duncan wrapped his hand in her straight hair, helping her find his rhythm, moving her back and forth. Then, as the first drops of his pre-come spilled free, he asked in a low whisper, "Do you like the way we taste together?"

She murmured an answer, her mouth still filled with his cock, her words all slurred around it. He stroked her fine, muscled back, feeling the cut lines of her muscles tensing and sliding beneath her skin. She swallowed harder, trying to take him all the way down her throat, trying to devour him. Pleasuring him as she vied for power.

It was in his head to turn her over onto her back, straddle her high up and feed his cock to her, inch by inch, the position helping her take it down her throat until her lips met the heated skin of his body. It was in his mind to roll her over the second before he came and explode onto her naked back, covering the hazy red welts with his semen. Covering her pain with his bliss.

But she surprised him, reared up when he was lost and almost coming, got him down on his back on the bed, with the belt in *her* hand. She had his arms bound above his head before he knew what was going on. She moved up him, as he'd imagined doing to her, and bestowed him with the gift of the split between her legs, positioning herself over his mouth in the way that would bring her the most satisfaction.

Her back still throbbed from the strokes he'd given her. The feel of his tongue probing her cunt combined with the pain and made her dizzy. That mixture of pain–pleasure had always haunted her, driving her to the darkest sexual back alleys, driving her into the arms of less-deserving lovers than him.

They were perfect together. He'd been on a similar quest: patronizing whores in every part of the world, learning from them, bringing his fantasies to life in the attic rooms of old hotels. Handing over the currency ahead of time and then taking out the props (handcuffs, riding crop, blindfold) that fit his latest craving. But no one had ever been able to take him where he needed to go, the highest pinnacle, the moment of blinding, white-hot fire that would ultimately satisfy his raging hunger.

And then this girl. The one who craved the opposite of his every fantasy. The one who needed to be taken as much as he needed to possess, who needed to feel the pain as much as he needed to inflict it. He'd searched for her endlessly, sometimes catching a glimpse in a club or bar late at night, or on the street—always different, chameleon-like. A silky-haired blonde in Paris, on her knees in an alley off the Seine, giving head to a man in a worn-out tuxedo. A young brunette beauty in Venice, whose amazing blue eyes flashed at him. He'd watched her from a gondola as her lover bent her over the bridge and fucked her. He'd listened breathlessly to the cries and moans that she'd made, watched her fingers gripping the cool stone of the bridge as if searching for purchase.

And then, finally, he'd found her in L.A., at After Dark. Or had she found him? In the larger pattern of things, there are no accidents. The prey is destined for its predator as the wheat is destined for the mill and the grape for the winepress. The victim seeks not to be consumed, but transformed. That was Yolanda's quest: to be transformed. She knew the only way to obtain pure essence was through distillation, a process that demanded intense heat. Heat to burn away all the impurities, to evaporate everything that diluted the essential element of her being.

And as she threw her head back and felt herself coming, as she moved back and climbed onto his cock and rode him, as she met his eyes and saw the glimmer there, saw that they were one, she knew she'd found him.

And, thus knowing, knew she'd never let him go.

Never Say Never

Rachel Kramer Bussel

I can only come when my legs are spread apart as wide as possible. It doesn't matter what else is going on at the time; if my legs are spread, I come so hard I feel like a rocket about to be zoomed into space, wild and breathing fire and out of control. I like the way my legs stretch and pull apart and cause all sorts of divine sensations in my cunt. Even the tiniest movements make my insides quiver and quake; sometimes I feel on the verge of tears, the sensations are that intense. Nothing else can compare. All of my partners have been more than happy to oblige. It's really the only thing that works with me. At least, that's what I thought.

Until Jesse.

One night, I was at a play party, a pretty quiet and slow one, which was fine with me. I decided to attend because it was the only game in town and I didn't really want to be home all alone, but I wasn't in the most sociable mood. I was alone, eating chips and gazing off into space, physically present—but mentally off in my own dream world.

"What are you into?"

Someone had just invaded my quiet little area, barging right up to me in such an aggressive way I had to look around to make sure we were at the same staid party that happens every month. We were, even though I almost never see women act so boldly there. They usually eye each other all night and make suggestive comments and then at the very last minute quickly ask if the other one wants to play, knowing that there's only time for the shortest of scenes.

I was impressed with her audacity. I knew her name, Jesse, because everyone knew her name. I'd never spoken to her and she'd never so much as glanced at me before that I could tell, but I guess she'd noticed me lurking around. Maybe she was more observant than I'd given her credit for. She didn't ask me first whether I was into her or wanted to play. I guess that was implied by the way I slouched against the wall, without trying to slink away or avert my eyes. Or maybe she was just one of those women filled with so much self-confidence that the idea of someone not wanting to play with her is completely foreign. In my case, her hunch was correct, but I didn't want to make myself seem that easy. I stood there staring coolly back at her. The body language of consent was all she was going to get.

"I said, what are you into?" she repeated, this time with an edge to her voice. I hadn't answered yet because I don't have a set answer, a one-size-fits-all play requirement; for me it really depends on the person, the setting, the context. It's an odd question to me too; how will I know what will work with her until I try it? So I gave her a broad but definite response.

"I don't know if this is what you're looking for, but I really like to come with my legs spread as far apart as they can be. That always works for me."

I didn't tell her it was the only thing that worked for me, didn't think I had to. She just looked at me; I couldn't read her gaze. She seemed slightly unpleased, but she just took my hand and led me into a room. She closed the door; I didn't look to see if she locked it, only half caring. I like my privacy too, even at a public play party.

"So I'm not quite sure I understand what you mean. Why don't you show me this fabulous way you like to come with your legs spread?"

I was sweating and my heart was pounding. She was acting friendly but I still felt intimidated, waiting for the other shoe to drop and her secretly nefarious intentions to be revealed. I was used to tops telling me what to do, not asking for things from me. Maybe in this case she was doing both. I liked her and was turned on but wasn't sure if I could follow her instructions. It's one thing to come alone, twisting and turning into all sorts of bizarre contortions to reach that pinnacle of pleasure, but doing it in front of another person, especially one who's demanding it, was going to be a bit daunting.

I quietly asked if she had a vibrator. She handed me a small but powerful black plug-in one. I gripped it tightly, noting the controls, then closed my eyes, afraid seeing her would affect me too much. I lay down on my back, spreading my legs wide. Then I turned it to the highest speed possible, the sound drowning out her breathing, and pressed it against myself. I felt my clit light up, straining for more contact, and spread my legs wider. I love how flexible I get when I'm aroused. I had my legs as wide apart as I could get them, when she came over towards me. She leaned over me, put her hands on my feet and pressed hard. Now I was totally split apart, the pain streaking down my thighs, twisting my pussy and making the vibrations that much more intense. I was having trouble breathing, but I didn't mind. She kept pushing, staring down at me like some devious X-rated aerobics instructor. I could imagine her saying "Feel the burn," as she kept bearing down on me, my cunt utterly exposed to her powerful eyes. I started to rock back and forth slightly, really getting into it, knowing that she was safely holding me, when the power stopped. She'd unplugged it somehow; I was so lost in my thighs and clit that I didn't notice until it all came to a grinding halt. I stared up at her beseechingly. She couldn't be making me stop now, she just couldn't.

"That's enough of that for now, I just wanted to see what you like. Very good. Now we're going to try something new," she said briskly, like she was my boss giving me a challenging new assignment.

I wanted to protest, but there was no time. She pulled me up and had me stand with my hands over my head. My heart was still beating fast, and I had no idea what was about to happen. She shackled my wrists above my head, and while they didn't feel uncomfortable, I found myself starting to squirm. She pushed me towards the wall, facing it, and didn't have to tell me to stay there. I was turned on but there was very little I could do about it besides pressing my cunt against the wall.

Then I felt her start to bind my ankles. I opened my mouth, but just held it open for a minute. What could I say? She obviously knew what she was doing and had a plan for me. It felt kind of good actually, the soft rope pressing into my taut ankles, yet I couldn't help wanting to spread my legs, even a little. All I could do at that point was rise up and down on my toes and wiggle fruitlessly against the ropes. When I tried that, she looked up at me with a severe expression, daring me to protest. When she'd finished with the last knot, she told me, "I think you'll change your mind, sweetheart, just wait and see." I had little choice on the waiting since I was now at her mercy.

I could feel myself getting wet, a liquid refutation of my wiggling protests. She leaned into my ear. "I'm going to spank you and whip you now, and you're going to like it, I can tell. I've heard about you, you little slut, acting all quiet and shy but I know what you really want. And it'll be all the better because I'm gonna make you come with those pretty legs pressed together as tight as can be. I know you want to show off, you want everyone to see your nice, wet pussy, and how far you can spread those legs. You're good at that, I already told you. But I'm not gonna let you show off that pussy or move those thighs, not this time."

With that, she surprised me yet again, leaning me over a padded bar that reminded me of the kind I used to leap over during gymnastics class. With my head leaning forward, I could open my eyes, but the view wasn't all that spectacular: the dusty beige floor tiles were about all I could make out. In the silence, I listened for clues, sweating and breathing rapidly. I felt a movement behind me and then her hand coming down hard on my ass. I jolted, pressing myself more tightly against the padded surface. She spanked me again, and continued, keeping a rapid rhythm that was getting me wetter and wetter. At some point I felt something new. I knew that it was no longer her hand but something much stronger making contact with me. The pain was a rush but I knew that it alone wouldn't be enough for me.

The rope cut into my ankles as I pressed them as far apart as they would go, which wasn't very far at all. I could only rock back and forth, stick my ass out further, but my legs wouldn't stretch in the way that I love them to. I felt torn between enjoying the delicious sensations my ass was receiving and wanting to move my legs apart. I wanted her to see and feel just how wet I really was. And then I heard a knock at the door. I sighed, not wanting to stop. She left my side to answer the door, and I heard a whispered conversation that I couldn't make out.

She returned with someone else, a stranger. I didn't get to hear her introduce herself either. Jesse did the speaking for both of them. "M is going to take over now, because I have something else I need to do." She didn't ask me, just stated it simply. Her tone was totally calm, verging on disinterested, and it made me want to show off for her, impress her. Jesse lifted me up, then moved the bench away. I wanted that bench, wanted to have something to lean on, something to help me keep my composure, to prevent me from free-falling, literally and figuratively. But I had to trust that Jesse knew what she was doing; she certainly seemed to as she had me stand up straight, my ankles still bound, my wrists hanging together in front of me.

She placed herself in front of me, her hand covering my pussy. I pressed against her, wanting to feel more contact. I was relaxing into this new sensation when I felt the first smack. It came much harder than Jesse's, pressing me into Jesse's hand and sending its vibrations through my whole body. I opened my eyes and looked up at Jesse, pleadingly. With her hand on my cunt, I wanted to spread my legs and slide her hot fingers into me, but of course that was impossible. Her fingers started working my clit, as the beating continued. I let out a little scream, wanting to move. "Oh, so you think you're going to come, do you? Is that possible, just from me playing with your nice juicy clit here, and M spanking you? Is it possible for you to come with those legs pressed so tightly together that it looks like you're trying to hold in your pee? I want you to press them even more tightly together, that's right." And with that she took her hand away and moved behind me. "Now, my dear, you are in for a little treat." I heard her open the door and let in our audience. I didn't mind, thinking maybe she'd undo my legs for this. But she had something else in mind.

"Now, my friends, here is Miss 'I-can-only-come-with-my-legs-spread-far-apart.' She prefers them spread all the way out, flung as far as they can go so her pretty little cunt is on display and she's taking up as much room as possible. She told me that's the only way she can come, but she agreed to let me play a little game to see if that's really true. You can place your bets with each other but I'm warning you now—I'm a sure thing." And then she sauntered back to me. "And just to make extra sure those legs stay put, I'm going to tie her up a bit more securely." And with that she slipped another piece of rope around me and tied me yet again, this time at the thighs. The rope pressed into that fleshy area, and I could barely stand it. Now I really couldn't move my legs and it was driving me mad. I wished she could at least tie me up with something between my legs to relieve some of this pressure she'd created.

She bent down to whisper in my ear, and for once her words were kind and soft, a surprise to me. "I'll make you come, sweetheart, don't you worry." And then she resumed her show for the crowd. "Now look at the way her legs are bound tight together, and yet she's still trying to spread them apart. See her pushing against them here, and here." She tapped me on the sides of my legs, Exhibits *A* and *B* of my struggle. "She thinks I can't make her come with her legs pressed so tightly against each other and her pussy all squeezed in there. Well, I've already told you who the odds are on." And then she took over where M had left off, and M took her position in front of me. I had little time to think as sharp, intense strokes fell on my ass, the pain of each settling in for only moments before another blow landed. I looked up at M to see her reaction but she stood there totally stoically, staring at me, like she was only there because Jesse had asked her to be. Her indifference maddened and excited me. Hers was the only face I could see, so I looked back at her. Then Jesse really started teasing me, using whatever had been sharply stinging my ass to do the same on the flesh right beneath it. I let out a long audible breath and scrunched up my face as I felt her move seemingly closer to my cunt with the whip, yet not close enough. I wanted something, anything, between my legs, or I was going to die right then and there.

I was squirming and wet and by that point not even sure what I wanted. I struggled against the ropes just to feel any sensation other than the pinpoints of pain on the backs of my thighs.

And then M, still looking quite dispassionate, leaned down and began licking my clit. She started off softly, and I restrained myself from pushing her head harder against me, knowing that Jesse wouldn't stand for such insubordination. As it was, I just grunted. Both of them sped up their paces, the blows falling harder and harder on my ass, my thighs, my back. M used her tongue like a sword, cutting this way and that, no longer gently licking but forcefully beating my clit with her tongue. Then she sucked it into her mouth, as if it were my nipple, her lips and then teeth wrapping around it. The ropes dug deeply into my thighs as I rocked back and forth, left and right, any way I could. M grabbed my hip, digging her nails into my flesh, and I screamed, coming in such a flash of heat and power and liquid that I almost knocked us all over. Jesse and M stepped aside and moved me into a corner, leaving me to recover, gasping as I leaned against the wall.

"Okay, ladies, thank you for coming." With that, Jesse ushered our guests out the door, a few grumbles coming from the poor suckers who'd bet on me as they forked over their cash.

Then Jesse stood staring down at me, a pitying look on her face. "You're a smart girl but you have a big, bratty mouth. You should learn to watch that. If you've taken anything away from tonight, besides a sore ass and that greedy pussy of yours, I hope it's that you should never, ever, say never when it comes to the way you can and can't come. You just might surprise yourself."

As she leaned down to undo the knots that had held my legs together so well, I couldn't help but agree.

Home Entertainment

Felix D'Angelo

The house is dark when I get home late; I'm wondering where you are. Maybe you went out for a drink with friends, or stepped out for a late dinner. It's especially strange, because your car's in the driveway. You might have gone to sleep early, but you always leave the light on for me.

Then I understand as I close the front door behind me and reach out to flick the light switch; the light's burned out. I would curse, but you're on me before I can.

You scare the shit out of me as you grab me and ram me against the wall, your hands pinning my wrists behind me. Then I recognize your voice, growling throatily in my ear: "Don't move," you tell me.

You let go of my hands and my arms hang limp at my sides.

I can smell you, your scent rich in the darkness. You cinch my wrists tight and push me harder against the wall; that's when I feel the cold steel of the knife.

You don't even ask; we've never negotiated this. That's why my cock swells unbidden as I feel you taking hold of my T-shirt and slicing it down the back. Two more slices across the sleeves, and it falls to ribbons behind me. I feel the flat of the knife pressing against my throat.

"Kick off your shoes," you order me. "And take off your pants."

I kick off my tennis shoes, unfasten my belt and unzip my pants. I step out of them and you grab my hair and pull my head back. The knife is at my throat again, but you don't need it to control me; my cock is so hard you could do anything you want.

"Into the bedroom," you growl, and shove me towards it.

Inside, candles are lit, a bizarrely romantic touch setting off the restraints affixed to each corner of the headboard and footboard. You spin me around and shove me backward, coming down hard on top of me and pinning me to the bed.

My wrists go easily into the restraints; I look up at you as you buckle them and click the small padlocks. You're wearing skintight stretch jeans and knee-high zip-up boots, a black leather top hugging your slim breasts with a silver zipper going down between them, all the way to your bare belly. Your long hair is pulled up in a severe bun.

You make short work of my ankles, affixing them to the bed frame as well. I lay there spread-eagled, helpless, staring up at you with my cock hard. You slide back on top of me, the knife glinting in the candlelight. You run it slowly up my thigh and gently tease the shaft of my hard cock with the tip.

"That was easy," you say. "I figured I'd have to at least suck you a little to get you hard."

I moan as you draw the tip of the knife up my body, over my stomach and chest. You touch it to my throat and I find myself wondering, fear gripping my chest, if it's sharp. Surely you know better than to play with a sharpened knife... don't you?

It's been a few days since I shaved, so I get my answer. You draw the edge of the blade over my cheek, and wipe your fingers over my upper neck. When you shove them into my mouth, I feel the tiny fragments of whisker that tell me you *don't* know better. With that knowledge comes a surge of arousal and a wave of fear. I look up into your eyes, frightened by the cold amusement I see there.

"Do exactly what I want," you whisper, "and we won't have a problem."

You sit up on the bed and unzip your leather top, peeling it away from your sweat-moistened breasts. Your nipples stand out dark and hard with arousal. Your freckled flesh shimmers with the candlelight as you toss the leather top away and bend forward over me.

"Suck them," you tell me.

I take your nipple into my mouth and gently begin to tongue it. "Harder!" you order, and I suck harder, biting slightly, suckling you hungrily and flicking my tongue faster over your nipples. You could do this for hours; I've done it to you for hours, making you endure torture you loved almost as much as you're loving this.

"You're going to make me come," you growl. "Without ever touching my pussy or my clit."

You can come from having your nipples sucked—if you're really, really turned on. I've only managed it once.

"I don't know if I can," I whisper.

"You better hope so," you say, and slip the knife into my mouth. I taste it, tangy and metallic. I look up into your face and you're smiling, but it's not a comforting smile. It's the smile of the predator, knowing what she wants and being prepared to take it.

You slip the knife out of my mouth. Now it's slick with my spittle. You guide one nipple back into my mouth and I start sucking it obediently.

You cradle my head in your arms, running the knife over my throat as you give me directions. "Now the other nipple...

lick them…tell me you want it," and I obey every command. I lose track of time, lost between your tits and struggling against the bonds that hold me. When you reposition yourself, centered over me, straddling my crotch, I suck harder as I feel you pressing the crotch of your stretch jeans against my cock.

"You want to fuck, don't you?" you whisper. "Keep doing it real good and we'll see."

I lose myself even deeper into your breasts, as you move your upper body back and forth, brushing the firm orbs over my face. The knife serves as a constant reminder of who's in control, as does the hard, insistent way you grind your spandex-sheathed crotch against my cock. But it's you who's losing control. You're mounting closer to orgasm, your body grinding harder against me, sweat glistening on your breasts and belly. You clutch my head tighter to your breasts, my mouth working on one nipple as you start playing with the other, pinching it between thumb and forefinger and rolling, the way you've taught me to do. You force your pussy harder against my cock, and I can tell the shaft is rubbing your clit.

"Keep sucking," you pant. "Keep sucking…don't you dare stop…."

And I do, desperately working my tongue over your nipple, sucking hard, the way you like it when you're going to come. You freeze up and I almost think you're not going to make it, but then your body relaxes, melting like an icicle all over me, and you press your upper body down hard, bearing me into the pillow as you force your nipple deep into my mouth, coming. Your crotch presses rhythmically against the long shaft of my cock, the spandex jeans abrading my sensitive flesh as you shudder on top of me.

When you're finished coming, you sit up, tugging your nipple out of my mouth.

"Well done," you say. "Think you deserve what's under these jeans?"

"I don't know," is all I can moan as you roll onto your side and shove your boot against my mouth.

"Pull it down," you tell me, guiding the leather-sheathed zipper between my lips.

I grab the zipper with my teeth, rocking back and forth as you pull your boot slowly up. When it's unzipped, you shove the heel into my mouth and tell me to grab hold.

And your boot comes sliding off, in my mouth, the grit of the floor against my tongue. You pluck it from me and toss it away, then repeat the procedure on the other foot. Then you make me take off your socks with my teeth. When you're barefoot, you kneel over me on the bed and unzip your stretch jeans.

You peel them off slowly, making me wait, making me savor every inch of your slim white hips as you display them to me in the flickering candlelight. You're not wearing anything underneath them, and your pussy is shaved smooth. You wriggle out of your jeans and shove the crotch against my face, letting me smell how turned on you've gotten.

"Still think you deserve a fuck?" you ask me.

"I don't know," I tell you.

"Let's find out," you say, and spread your legs over my face.

Your pussy tastes strong, overwhelming. I slide my tongue between your smooth lips and find your clit as you press your crotch down onto my face. My cock throbs hard at my other end, but the most you do is wrap your hand around it, breathe your warm breath over it, and slide the knife up the shaft, then back down, caressing my balls with the tip. You laugh. "You can't wait to get this in there, can you?" you ask me. "Eat my pussy good enough and we'll see." Then you grind your crotch down harder on my face, pressing me into the pillow as you spread your thighs over me. I focus on your clit, tasting your juices flowing into my mouth as you start to rhythmically fuck my face. You're moaning softly, like you're going to come a second time, which you almost never do. But now, it's unmistakable. You're forcing your pussy harder against my mouth, demanding more, insisting that I lick you harder. And I follow every instruction you give me, feeling your knife against my balls and moving up to the tip of my cock. But when you're ready to come, the knife disappears and I feel your mouth, hear you moaning as you climax, unable to stop your hunger for my cock—betraying yourself as you take it into your mouth and suck on it as you pump your hips, forcing my tongue harder onto your clit with every spasm of your climax. When you pull your mouth away, you're done with teasing. You lift your pussy off my face, looking down at me as I smell the remnants of your arousal smeared across my lips and chin. You tower over me, breathing hard. You straddle my crotch and put your knife to my throat again, the lips of your pussy spreading slightly around the head of my cock.

"I think you've earned it," you say, and push yourself down onto me.

My back arches and I moan so loud I'm afraid the neighbors will hear. My eyes go wide as I explode with sensation, your pussy enveloping me, tight and powerful. My hips rise to meet yours as you pump down onto me, and we fuck each other with mutual thrusts that hit hard when our hipbones meet. We're both going to be bruised tomorrow, but I don't care. I fuck you harder, panting wildly as I get closer to orgasm—and then I'm coming, deep inside you, feeling my cock surge with pleasure as I fill you.

Squirming on top of me, your crotch still pressed hard to mine, my cock softening inside you, you set the knife on the bedside table.

"You earned it," you tell me, your face nuzzling up against the smooth patch on my chin.

Good Things Come

Iris N. Schwartz

Last night, Helena found herself smacking the lipstick-red telephone receiver against her moist and darkening pussy lips, simply because a voice on the other end of the line had commanded her to do so. Tonight, she was tied with gold velvet scarves to an antique chair belonging to the owner of that voice, and she feared—or hoped—that a Princess receiver might be the most banal object to be imposed on her delicate parts.

The man who possessed the chair and the voice, Philip—gray-maned, lush-lipped, tight-dungareed—had been gone for quite some time from this ascetically appointed room. Just how long she didn't know, as Helena had been stripped of her micrometer watch minutes after her entrance. Her timepiece, claret suede miniskirt, sheer stockings, fuchsia garter belt, satin-trimmed camisole, black Wonderbra, over-the-knee lace-up boots, even the silver hoop earrings and sterling belly chain she had purchased for the occasion, all had been removed.

Helena had been divested of all these by a woman who had first transported her, one powerful hand gripping Helena's wrist, to a narrow cage at the end of an otherwise empty hallway. The woman had backed her against the bars, breathing softly against much of Helena's body while slowly removing all clothing and accessories. Then the woman, who had been wordless the entire time, locked the cage behind herself and left Helena to wait, naked on the cold iron floor, for who knew how long, for who knew what. Helena had waited, excited and tearful, feeling perspiration gather under her heavy breasts in the metallic air.

Minutes later the woman returned, this time with a black, spaghetti-strap chemise, which she placed next to Helena with the blasé efficiency of a nurse tossing an open-backed hospital gown to a patient. A patient propped up on an examining table. A patient with no knowledge of the medical procedures to follow.

Now Helena was waiting, herself wordless, having been led by Philip to a behemoth chair in a stark, parquet-floored room, empty but for this chair and a king-sized brass bed against the far right wall. Helena wondered when she would get to that bed, when Philip would allow her to move her limbs and exult in spread-eagled comfort and space, revel in the cool alloy against her flushed, tingling skin.

For all Helena knew, this Philip was a thief and a sadist who got his kicks by stealing a lonely woman's jewelry and underthings, then leaving her to languish, bound to a medieval chair. He would let her be discovered—near naked, poorer and sexually frustrated, still—by the building superintendent, or any service person lucky enough to open the door.

Ah! It dawned on Helena, as if she were a patient seeing the grim face of her doctor walking slowly towards her: *This is what I'm supposed to think!* She twisted her stiff hips and stared down at her silk-covered form. Helena felt her nipples harden and the areolas pucker at the thought of a stranger finding her, her breasts and pelvis thrust forward from this now sweat-dappled chair, her legs and arms tied with the same luxuriously soft but sturdy fabric.

At once a rosy blush overtook her pallor. How could a man unknown to her just two nights before have the authority to fill her heart with such trepidation, such anger, such out-and-out...willingness to comply? Then Helena understood that all this, too, must be what Philip wanted. Must be what she wanted. She was tired of being the boss: the cool boss, the smart boss, the head-like-a-Grolier's and heart-like-a-tundra boss, the boss at work and the boss in bed. She was tired of having to know, of having to pretend she knew when she didn't, of having to pretend it was fine when most people didn't know as much or even try to know as much as she did. When they didn't try to please and excel as she did—at work and in bed. She was tired of it all. And she was too damn young to be this tired.

Helena took a deep breath. Still no sign of Philip. She hoped he'd be back soon, to do with her what he would, soon. At least she had told two friends of her plans, and the precise location as well.

A chill coursed through Helena's barely attired body, depositing goose bumps everywhere, from her fragile arms to her lengthening nipples, from her solid buttocks to her soft belly and, finally, to her shockingly moist, honey-redolent pussy and inner thighs. Philip could do worse than leave her, helpless, naked, alone: He could kill her. He could do worse than kill her: He could rape her, knife her, and then leave her, crumpled, broken, and bleeding—no longer beautiful—to live out her life with jagged scars defining her person as well as her memories.

Yet she did not scream. No scarf covered her lips, no ball filled her mouth. Helena was free to bellow for help. Instead, she sat there, bound at wrists and ankles, upper lip touched with perspiration, lower lips drenched with juices of desire, waiting for Philip. When at last he walked into the room, gray hair loose about his naked shoulders, full lips pursed with determination, ropes on one muscled arm and chains on the other, Helena knew she was ready and willing. As Philip nodded first at her and then at the brass bed, Helena experienced the betrayal of her juices seeping further onto her upper thighs. She sighed—extravagantly, involuntarily. Philip would be just what the patient ordered.

Helena watched as her leonine captor tied heavy ropes to the brass posts at the foot of the bed; she panted as he strode to the head of the bed and wound silver chain securely to those posts. Her wrists and ankles nearly chafed with anticipation.

Then Philip was behind the antique chair, his thick mane cascading over her face as he bent to undo the scarves. Helena was engulfed by his scent, warm but severe, akin to a dusting of cinnamon on steel.

Philip grabbed her right wrist and pulled her to his bed. He threw her onto cool white sheets. She tried not to look at him as he roughly tied her ankles and wound cold chain over her wrists, tugging and wrapping the chains until she sat with her back stick-straight against the brass headboard, her legs obscenely splayed. Helena's dominant spread her thighs with both hands and thrust a finger into her pussy, making deep, circular motions. Much too soon he withdrew his finger, wiped it on her thigh, and smirked.

That's when she saw it: small, silver, glinting like his polished brass finials. Before Helena could open her mouth to scream, Philip waved the knife he had pulled from his back pocket. *Oh, this is it. This is what happens to bad girls like me.* Philip ran the tip through the front of the spaghetti-strapped gown, slitting and separating the material from her in one motion. Then he tossed knife and gown onto the floor.

Helena looked down at her body: no blood, no marks. Now she screamed. Philip smacked her pussy and clit with his open palm—once, twice. Before he could make it a third time Helena succumbed. She gushed on Philip's hand, hot liquor running onto and flooding his sheets. She was screaming still but not from fear. She didn't know if he was angry with her, but he stretched and twisted her swollen nipples with one hand while alternately smacking her clit and jamming fingers into her with the other. Helena couldn't think, could barely breathe; all she could do was come and scream, naked, spread wide, in front of this silent, imperious stranger.

And when she stopped screaming, at which point he ceased this delicious infliction, Philip unzipped his jeans and, bringing his crotch up to her face, rammed his handsome, coral-hued cock into her waiting mouth. Only after pulling out in time to spray her face with steamy, pearly come did he release her to wander off to a shower and her clothes. The last thing Helena saw before stepping into the hallway was his assistant removing the sheets. The woman would soon fit crisp new ones onto the bed, readying this highly proficient doctor of discipline for the next patient.

Melinda

Mitzi Szereto

It hurt at first. But then it got better. Just like they told her it would. Melinda had never considered allowing anyone to tie her up. The idea of handing her body over to another person—of relinquishing her control and her womanhood to people she barely knew—had no place on her list of Things to Do Before I Die. Of course there were a lot of things Melinda would never have considered doing before the night she went to the annual company Christmas party, unescorted and conspicuously alone.

The event started off like all the Christmas parties that had gone before, with nearly everyone in attendance parading their dates before their colleagues, their overly loud laughter and too-bright smiles making Melinda feel more out of the social fray than usual. Not fond of large gatherings, she immediately regretted not having coerced her gay friend Joel into coming along with her. He was always a handy escort when she found herself in a pinch, particularly since he knew just when to fade into the background. But tonight Melinda didn't want to be bogged down with a date, bogus or otherwise. She wanted to be available, just in case. She'd even brought along her credit card to splurge on a room in the swanky hotel where the party was being held. Why, she could see the misty green landscape of Hyde Park from the window already!

As it happened, the only view of Hyde Park Melinda ended up being treated to on this wet December evening was the one from the hotel lobby. Evidently the creative head of corporate advertising she'd had her eye on lately had far more interesting things to do with his Saturday night than spend it with the office gadabouts, unlike Melinda, who really didn't have anything else to do on this rainy Saturday night. It was either attending the company Christmas party or cuddling up with the cat to watch yet another television documentary featuring a rhapsodic David Attenborough narrative on the sex lives of creepy-crawly things that live under rocks.

At the moment, Melinda was more concerned about her own sex life, which had definitely hit the skids. This recent downward sexual spiral had gained some unwanted momentum thanks to Melinda's involvement with a man from her gym. In retrospect, she probably should have realized from the start that anyone with that many muscles spent most of his time lifting weights and none on building up a career. It didn't take long for Melinda to decide she could easily forfeit all that hard defined male flesh in return for a steady bed partner with a steady salary and something to talk about beside abs and pecs. For after only a couple of steamy sessions, Blake and his weight-lifting paraphernalia had virtually moved into her tiny flat. Granted, they were pretty good steamy sessions as steamy sessions go, but they were by no means fulfilling enough to warrant her financial support of the man—not even if his tongue *was* as muscular and rippling as the rest of him! Whether she was at her most exhausted or sexually apathetic, one dose of Blake's hardworking tongue between her thighs would be enough to make Melinda forget the pile of paperwork waiting for her at the office. Too bad the rest of Blake wasn't as industrious as his tongue.

As she stood by the bar sipping spicy Christmas punch from a plastic cup and nodding the occasional hello to a familiar face, Melinda's glittery evening bag burned an embarrassing reminder against her hip. The unused VISA card that had been placed inside it with such careful premeditation before she left home for the party now made her feel like a fool. At the time it had seemed like a terribly sophisticated thing to do. But as her meticulously made-up eyes swept across the crowd of revelers searching for the one face she most wanted to see, Melinda realized that the expensive French perfume lavished behind her ears and on the insides of her thighs had been wasted, along with the outrageous sum of money that had gone toward the purchase of her new black dress, which had looked *so-o-o* sexy when she'd tried it on in the shop. So profound was her disappointment on what should have been a festive occasion that she considered leaving. However, all this changed when her crestfallen gaze met that of a dark-featured young man who looked as out of place as she felt.

Perhaps it was the expression of contemplative amusement in his smoky Eastern eyes that set him so apart from the others in the noisy hotel banquet room. This and the fact that he appeared to be the only male in attendance not drinking himself into a state of obnoxiousness or risking his teeth on the dried-out chicken wings, made his presence all the more noticeable. Or at least it did to Melinda, who found his aloofness strangely appealing. This was not a man who needed to call attention to himself. And neither, for that matter, did his fair-skinned female companion. For he stood in a gaudily decorated corner elbow-to-elbow and thigh-to-thigh with the most stunning woman Melinda had ever seen: an ephemeral white-blonde with eyes as amber as a cat's and the stealthy mouse-baiting movements to go along with them. How was Melinda to know that she would be that mouse?

Although not usually the sort to be physically attracted to her own gender, Melinda could not keep from staring at the feline young woman whose skin looked like it had been made from finely crushed pearls. She found it equally difficult to keep from staring at the café-au-lait young man whose conflicting features were every bit as striking as those of his companion. Melinda knew she was being fairly obvious about it, but she didn't mind if the couple noticed her interest. In fact, she secretly wanted them to. The contrast the pair made against the raucous backdrop of braying corporate types populating the area gave Melinda the impression they had wandered into the party by mistake or else out of boredom and the desire for a free drink. Either that or the Christmas punch had been more punched-up than usual and she had begun to hallucinate. Nevertheless, there was nothing at all hallucinatory about the sudden rush of moisture soaking the gusset of the black silk panties Melinda wore beneath her dress.

No one had spoken in the taxi. The only sounds were those of the London rain pattering teasingly against the vehicle's rolled-up windows and the ever-present *chig-chig-chig* of the diesel engine as the taxi made its way north toward Mill Hill. By now the drunken hilarity of the holiday celebrants had faded to a distant memory in Melinda's ears. Her breath grew heavy and increasingly ragged as she found herself being pleasantly squeezed between the two party crashers in the taxi's generous back seat, the sexually charged warmth of their bodies hinting at the delightful things to come, as did the flirtatious dance of their fingertips upon her opening thighs. Melinda had not said good-bye to her coworkers or informed them of her impetuous decision to accompany the mysterious couple to wherever they happened to be taking her on this soggy December evening. This was probably unwise, but tonight Melinda did not want to be her practical and reliable old self. Tonight she wanted to be someone else: the kind of someone who didn't care about things like caution.

The man and woman pressing themselves so provocatively against Melinda's hips and thighs had shown no sign of knowing their fellow partiers, which confirmed her suspicion that they had not been invited. Although why anyone would have wanted to crash a boring company Christmas do was a mystery. Much as it was a mystery why, from out of a roomful of stunning females, Melinda, who did not classify herself as being in the drop-dead gorgeous league, should have been singled out as she stood drinking punch in her brand-new black cocktail dress—one indistinguishable from all the other black cocktail dresses being worn. She grew hotter and wetter by the minute at the thought of what would be done to her after the taxi had dropped them at their destination. Tonight Melinda would be made to feel anything but average.

Within half an hour's time she found herself with her arms drawn back and bound with deftly executed expertise in a complex macramé of silken cord that even she would have agreed was a work of art in itself, had she been able to see behind her. Although perhaps it was just as well Melinda could not, since she would have shrieked with embarrassment at the sight of her unfolded buttocks and the lubricated pink plug of latex being inserted between them.

Masculine fingers formed dark fans across Melinda's fleshy rear cheeks as their smoky-eyed owner's female companion dropped onto her haunches to place the intrusive object inside the wriggling backside before her. In her present state of restraint, Melinda's hips were the only thing she could move. Kicking out with her feet was impossible: the braided length of cord looping around her ankles had been woven into the elaborate network of knots trapping her arms behind her, forcing Melinda into a pose of helpless subservience. Considering the circumstances, she found it curious not to be feeling any fear when she could do nothing to act in her own defense.

"Relax, Melinda," the man advised matter-of-factly as he checked her bonds. "Allow yourself to get used to the pain. Your reward will be so much greater."

"Don't fight it," agreed his female partner, placing a not-too-gentle cat's bite upon Melinda's flinching right buttock as emphasis. "You'll only make it harder for yourself."

Despite the reassurances of this appealing couple in whose hands she had perhaps foolishly placed herself, Melinda's instincts took over and she tried to eject the foreign presence. Her efforts proved futile, however, for the object refused to budge thanks to a unique design that thwarted even the most determined attempts to expel it. The more force she used, the more the latex filled her, expanding like a dry sponge in liquid until Melinda finally came to accept the fact that she had lost all ability to control what was being done to her body. There could be no going back for her now.

During all this time, not a word of protest was put forth by the couple's helpless captive. Melinda's mouth had already been fitted with a gag of sorts: a blue silk kerchief that would have looked more appropriate fluted to a crisp point in a gentleman's coat pocket than in the lipstick-smeared mouth of a bound and naked female at the complete sexual mercy of two individuals whose names she neither knew nor had bothered to ask. Speaking of which, how did the man know her name? Melinda was certain she had not told him or the woman. Actually, she had made a point not to tell them much of anything.

"Everyone has to have a first time."

The soft feminine purr startled Melinda, whose recent acceptance of her circumstances had not as yet extended to her latex intruder. So involved had she become in the act of ridding herself of its offending presence that her muscles were as tightly knotted as her bonds. Suddenly she realized how absurdly self-defeating it was to be struggling like this. Deferring at last to the couple's advice, Melinda tried to relax. She closed her eyes and began to breathe deeply through her nostrils, willing the tension to leave her body until all that remained was a fluttering in her chest from her wildly beating heart and an increasingly wild thudding from her vulva.

Melinda felt the amber-eyed woman's breath blowing a hot caress against her buttocks and she sighed into her silken gag. Having managed to calm down a bit, she was surprised to discover that what was being done to her did not feel at all unpleasant. On the contrary, the cleverly designed series of ridges she'd observed on the surface of the plug when it was held before her before disappearing in a pink blur behind, gave rise to thoughts and desires she would never have admitted to aloud. In the privacy of her mind Melinda caught herself wishing that the object penetrating her was not made of bloodless latex, but of hard male flesh—the engorged heated flesh she had been made to sample before her lips were fitted with the blue kerchief. She could still taste the dark-featured young man's slippery fluids in her mouth, along with the sweeter tang of his partner, whose moist female folds Melinda's tongue had likewise been called upon to please before its capacity to do so had been temporarily stifled.

While pondering what it might be like to be used this way by the nameless man whose hands held her open to the latex, Melinda's thoughts drifted toward such a seduction being undertaken by someone she actually knew, or at least saw nearly every day. Although she'd never confided her feelings to even her closest friends, Melinda had been suffering from a yearlong infatuation with a workmate—the one who had been absent from the Christmas party and for whom Melinda would have gladly forfeited a week's salary in exchange for a hotel room, Hyde Park view or not! Unfortunately Caleb worked in a different department a world away from her own, which only made it harder for Melinda to come up with legitimate-sounding excuses to seek him out during office hours. She was a numbers cruncher and he was a creative genius, two factors that didn't do much to bring them together.

Getting a man into her bed had never been a difficult task for Melinda. However, all that changed with Caleb, whose oblivious demeanor shook her self-confidence. Perhaps she wasn't his type. Maybe he wanted a woman who looked like a celebrity. Maybe if genetics had blessed her with a few more credits on the impossibly gorgeous side of the ledger, she might have made an effort to strike up a conversation in the canteen or in the courtyard when Caleb drifted outside for a smoke. The problem was, every time Melinda got ready to initiate a casual encounter, someone else would beat her to it, usually another female whose physical attributes and in-your-face sexuality far outweighed Melinda's own. Caleb was probably too young for her anyway. For all she knew, he might even be gay. At least this was what Melinda told herself whenever Caleb turned in her direction only to look straight through her as his lips sucked the smoke through the filtered tip of his cigarette.

Caleb's impervious features shattered into red-hot fragments of pain as the young woman attached a pair of small metal clips to Melinda's upstanding nipples. The effect was like tiny teeth biting into the rubbery points and Melinda shuddered violently, prompting a disapproving *tsk-tsk* from her female tormenter, who readjusted the clips so they nipped even more cruelly into the sensitive flesh. Melinda resumed the deep nasal breathing that had worked so well to calm her before and the pain in her nipples began to recede, giving way to a vexing heat. The same heat made itself felt when another pair of metal clips were clamped onto Melinda's hairless vaginal lips.

Like the silent young woman wielding these bizarre tools of pleasure, Melinda had been shaved to a virginal plain almost the moment after stepping across the threshold of this innocuous-looking Mill Hill house, leaving nothing secret and no sensation muted. Finding herself confronted with a safety razor had been quite a shock; she was briskly twisted and contorted until every hair both topside and rear had been hunted down and excised out of existence. Had it been the man wielding the blade rather than his pearly skinned collaborator, Melinda would have been too mortified to go through with the evening. Now, as the metal teeth of the clips sank provocatively into her intimate flesh and pain and pleasure blended into one, she knew she was ready for anything.

Melinda giggled into her gag at the thought of her tipsy colleagues back at the party, the highlight of their evening the free-flowing liquor and the equally free-flowing office gossip, none of which was likely to include her. Good old reliable Melinda, every corporation's wet dream. You could always count on her to stay late and finish the job. After all, she had nowhere important to run off to. There were no Calebs waiting for her at the pub or at that romantic new Italian restaurant with candles and Chianti on the tables; nor were there any bottles of California Chardonnay chilling in the fridge for later when they went back to her place. Never would these party-goers have imagined the sexy scenario taking place a few miles to the north—a scenario featuring a pair of expertly twittering tongues acting in symphonic harmony upon the innermost contours of Melinda's clipped-open labia. Of course this wouldn't be the first time she'd been underestimated!

Glancing down at the dark and light heads paying homage to her shaved sex, Melinda shook with the desire to touch this anonymous man and woman who had entered her life only hours ago. She wanted to feel their beautiful faces with her fingertips as their tongues worked with such artistry on her clitoris and its moist surroundings. But part of the bargain for her pleasure had been the loss of any control over what was being done to her. The gym-toned muscles in Melinda's arms and shoulders ached with frustration, much as they had ached earlier when she crouched on her knees before the bared genitals of her expectant hosts, whose orchestration of her oral movements inspired Melinda's tongue to a boldness she never knew it possessed. Yes, perhaps she had even underestimated herself.

It had been easier with the man, who thrust his penis to and fro in her mouth like one might in a vagina. Keeping hold of Melinda's chin-length chestnut hair, he pumped her open mouth until she thought her jaw would break, exacting punitive glances against her throat before finally emptying himself on her tongue with a sharp cry. For the first time in her life Melinda did not experience the urge to spit out a man's pleasure. Instead she wondered if the aloof Caleb would taste as sweet as this dark stranger who had forced himself upon her surprisingly eager mouth. "How lovely you are," he replied afterward in a husky whisper, leaning down to kiss Melinda's sticky lips before surrendering her to the amber-eyed female waiting with impatience at his side. Melinda had nearly forgotten about the other woman, so mesmerized had she been by her unquestioning submission to the man towering above her humbly posed form. However, she would promptly learn that his delicately featured sidekick was not the sort to let herself be forgotten.

Performing orally on another woman would be far more complicated than the straightforward techniques needed with a man, particularly since the recipient was no shrinking violet about making her desires known. Melinda found her hair being grasped ruthlessly, the expensively cropped chestnut strands almost ripped from the roots. “Get to it, Melinda!” the woman ordered with a cavalier toss of her white-blonde head, her characteristic kittenish purr now a caustic bark.

Melinda felt a forbidden tingle between her thighs at hearing her name uttered in conjunction with such a demand. The tingle gained in intensity, reaching near-orgasmic proportions when the young woman proceeded to rub her shaved and fragrant mound against Melinda’s lips until she arched her cat’s spine in orgasm. Although she had never previously had sex with her own gender, Melinda was not too shy to thrust her tongue inside her partner’s cream-filled vagina at the moment of her own climax, which had been achieved with no physical means but the ghostly sensations of the pair of tongues that had gone before. It reminded her of the stealthy orgasms she experienced while asleep which, upon awakening, would be followed by the discovery of her hands situated in innocent repose at her sides.

Melinda reflected often on that night of self-discovery in Mill Hill. Although she wouldn’t have minded repeating the occasion, she hadn’t made contact again with the man and woman responsible for giving her so much pleasure. The temptation to flag down a taxi and pay them a visit was one that became harder and harder to resist, especially since she had jotted down the street number of their house upon arriving back at her flat. But Melinda didn’t believe they would be there when she arrived. The house had had a temporary feel to it, as if the occupants were just using the place for a quick layover on their way to other adventures, which probably included other Melindas. From what she could recall out of the dizzying erotic haze she’d been in, the house had offered little in the way of furnishings—not that Melinda had been particularly interested in interior design that evening! Well, perhaps such things were best left as treasured memories, since it seemed doubtful that the overwhelming intensity of sensation she had been subjected to at the controlling hands of these two nameless and exotic strangers would ever be repeated. Even so, Melinda did not feel at all regretful. The dark young man and his amber-eyed companion had jolted her out of the humdrum dregs of daily life and taught her about her body's ability to achieve pleasure—a pleasure gained through restraint and pain. She had heard about people who got off on such sexual kinks, but had never bought into the pleasure-pain myth. Until now.

By the time she returned to the office after the Christmas break, Melinda had convinced herself that the couple had never existed. What had happened could only have taken place in her mind—a vivid erotic fantasy no doubt inspired by her yearlong infatuation with Caleb. As she settled in for the first work week of the New Year, she was surprised to find among all the pre-holiday clutter on her desk a tiny box covered in expensive wrapping paper. She first thought it must be a late Christmas gift, and she searched for an accompanying card. "Do you happen to know who left this on my desk?" Melinda called out to her assistant when her efforts to locate a card proved futile. A highly detail-oriented person, it annoyed Melinda when holiday gifts were not given on time.

"It was there when I came in this morning," came the assistant's unhelpful answer.

Melinda turned the little package every which way, puzzling over its contents. The box looked like the kind that usually contained earrings or a pendant. Not in the habit of wearing much jewelry, Melinda relied on her trusty pearl earrings for most situations, especially since joining the conservative ranks of corporate management. She had never been what anyone would have called a flashy person. She hoped this mysterious gift would be something she could use, because if the giver hadn't bothered to leave a card, it was also unlikely a sales receipt had been enclosed for the return of the item.

Melinda waited for her assistant to leave before taking a letter opener to the attractive wrapping paper. She could not understand why her hands were trembling over something so ridiculously mundane as a pair of earrings; she could barely manage the elementary task of prying off the little lid. All at once Melinda cried out with remembered pain, for lying incongruously upon a dainty square of cotton was a pair of metal clips. They looked identical to the metal clips that had been clamped to her nipples and vulva not three weeks ago. But surely that was impossible!

Melinda felt herself growing wet at the unexpected reappearance of the clips, and she squeezed her thighs together to calm the phantom sensations taking place between them. Her face burned with embarrassment as she wondered who in the office might have been privy to those lascivious events. A folded square of paper had been tucked halfway beneath the bed of cotton and she plucked it out. To her frustration, it provided no clue as to the identity of her bondage-minded gift giver. All it read was *Tonight*, along with a Maida Vale address. The note had been penned in a meticulous hand, the execution of the letters so tightly controlled and precise that Melinda could feel again the intricate weave of that silken cording. It was all she could do not to relieve herself with her fingers right there at her desk.

With the same sense of destiny she'd experienced on her way to Mill Hill on the rainy evening of the company Christmas party, Melinda took a taxi to the address on the note, the distinctive *chig-chig-chig* of the diesel engine adding an erotic sense of déjà vu to the occasion. The driver deposited her at the wrought-iron gate of a charming ivy-covered mews house, whose lace curtained windows were illuminated by a gentle light from within. Melinda thought she saw a tall shadow move past the one nearest the door, although she could not tell whether the shadow belonged to a man or a woman.

Ever so slowly Melinda made her way up the cobbled walk, taking a perverse pleasure in prolonging the moment before she would at last come face-to-face with the person or persons who had summoned her. For it had, indeed, been a summons she'd received. The handsomely painted front door opened before she could ring the bell.

"Hello, Melinda."

Melinda gasped aloud as the wetness that had been plaguing her ever since she had unwrapped her Christmas gift that morning soaked the gusset of her blue silk panties. She had specifically chosen to wear them this evening because they were the same shade of blue as the silk kerchief the couple from Mill Hill had used to bind her mouth. Standing before Melinda was the impervious young man who had occupied her thoughts and been the inspiration for her orgasms for the past year, the man she assumed never noticed her, who looked right through her as if she were invisible. But he was not doing so now. Instead the lips she had so often observed sucking the smoke through the filter tip of his cigarette formed a sardonic smile.

Caleb stepped forward, a safety razor held ready in his right hand. "You can't imagine how long I've been waiting for this," he replied softly.

"And she's definitely worth the wait, darling," came a familiar female voice. Melinda felt a sudden shift in the air as the feline presence of the young woman who had seduced her bound figure came into focus, followed by her smoky-eyed male conspirator.

"I understand you have already met my good friends Stephanie and Naveen?" Caleb looked deliberately into Melinda's astonished eyes, as if the question needed no answer.

Naveen's café-au-lait fingertips reached forward to stroke Melinda's cheek. "Wasn't it thoughtful of Caleb to have invited us to the company Christmas party?"

Caleb's smile widened. "Oh, but the party is only just beginning."

For Emphasis

Becky Chapel

"How can this woman be a famous novelist?" Gemma wondered as she circled *sparkling* for the sixteenth time. When she came upon the seventeenth use of the word, she set her red pen down angrily and picked up her phone. The novelist's home number was supposed to be used in emergencies only, but Gemma decided this counted. There was no way she could continue reading through this drivel without some sort of explanation. Or at the very least, an apology. Had the woman been on Xanax when she wrote the book? Had she been drunk? Was she simply seeing how far she could go before even her most die-hard fans refused to buy her work?

"Jill Baxton," the author said, surprising Gemma slightly by answering the phone herself. She'd thought she'd have to go through at least one barrier before reaching the writer. Didn't most famous people have handlers?

"Good evening, Ms. Baxton. This is Gemma Howard. I'm your new editor." Gemma waited until the novelist said, "Oh, yes, Melissa told me about you. I hear that you're good."

I hear that you're not, Gemma seethed in her head. *I hear that you're overrated and overpaid.* Aloud she said, "I'm a little confused by your manuscript."

"Confused in what way?"

"Did you mean to use the word *sparkling* seventeen times in chapter one of *Flowers for Her*? Or was the word a placeholder?" The sneer vibrated deep in her voice. Gemma relished the words and the silence that followed.

After a moment, the novelist said, "I used it for emphasis. That's my style. Melissa assured me that you'd read enough of my previous work to know how I write."

Without commenting on the statement, Gemma read the author's words back to her, "'She wore a sparkling necklace.' 'The fountain sparkled.' 'The champagne sparkled in the glasses.' 'Her eyes sparkled when she looked at him.' 'Each movement sparkled as she made her way toward her new love—'"

The novelist interrupted, saying, "I understand your point. Why don't you come to my place and bring the novel with you? We can edit the section together."

This suggestion caught Gemma off guard, but she quickly agreed, hung up the phone, grabbed the manuscript, and headed for the subway. What had she expected to gain from her phone call? She wasn't sure. She simply found that she no longer had it inside herself to coddle these people. There were so many up-and-coming novelists struggling to have their books even read by publishing houses. How could someone who'd reached the very top churn out such weak writing? That's what disturbed her the most.

But now, in transit, she found herself feeling slightly insecure about the situation. If she truly offended the author, the woman could without a doubt have her fired. There was no way her company would keep her on staff against the wishes of such a best-selling name. What she ought to have done was open a bottle of tequila—also kept on hand for dire emergencies—and drink as she read. That would have soothed her psyche enough for her to ignore the pathetic nonsense on the page. Now, what had she gotten herself into? This was just like Gemma—shooting off at the mouth without thinking. Yes, she was generally calm in the workplace, but in her private life, she acted first and dealt with the repercussions later. Never before had her wild side affected her job…never until now.

She tried to find her center as she moved out of the subway and up the steps. How should she behave when she arrived? Meek and apologetic—that seemed appropriate. She was simply trying to help after all, right? Perhaps, if she softened her critiques, the woman wouldn't tell her boss about the unorthodox phone call. Man, why the fuck was she even here? Out at night, just asking for trouble. That was easy to answer: The author's invitation had surprised her. She hadn't been able to think about the proper response. All she'd wanted to do when she called was vent, and look where that had gotten her.

Upon arriving at the designated address, she was even more surprised. The novelist's apartment was on Christopher Street in the Village, in a very non-best-seller type of building. When the woman opened the door, Gemma saw to her continued surprise that there was nothing in the room beyond except for a pair of handcuffs and the novelist, herself, clad entirely in black vinyl. The woman was pretty, much prettier than the pictures on the backs of her book jackets, where she appeared soft-edged and overly posed. In person, she was striking and lovely. Gemma felt even more insecure as the novelist looked at her. Again she wondered to herself, why was she here?

The women looked at each other for a long time in total silence.

"I don't like to be criticized," the novelist finally said before motioning for Gemma to enter the apartment and then shutting the door behind her. "If you want to continue to work for me, we need to get a few things straight."

Here was the perfect opportunity for Gemma to apologize profusely and save her job. Yet before she could even speak, Jill walked to Gemma and tilted her chin upward with one hand. "Do you understand me?" the author asked.

No, in truth, Gemma did not. A flutter of excitement worked through her, as she realized that the author was about to kiss her. How was that even possible? Jill's lips found Gemma's own and kissed her hard. Then, as Gemma stood there, trembling, the author undressed her in a few quick moves, discarding her simple outfit on the floor. Without a single word, the writer had handcuffed Gemma's wrists behind her neck. Gemma was awed. The woman was powerful, that much was clear. If she put this sort of power into her writing, her books would be brilliant. Gemma thought about saying this out loud, but she didn't have the time or the nerve.

The novelist moved closer. Suddenly, she had a crop in her hand. She was a magician, Gemma decided, swallowing down on a wave of fear. Everything was happening so quickly, the editor felt as if she couldn't focus her attention on the correct part of the story—the story that she found herself starring in.

"You said 'seventeen,'" the novelist told her. It wasn't a question, but Gemma nodded anyway. "We'll start with that."

She didn't have to stay. She could scream, could insist that Jill undo her this instant. She could pound on the wall, kick against it with her feet until some neighbor decided to call the cops. Or she could take it. Wasn't that the best solution? Wasn't that what she most wanted?

Gemma hadn't known pain like this before, shattering, demolishing, freeing. She was bent, twisted, pulled over the woman's knees to receive the blows. She kept quiet as long as she was able, and then, when she wasn't, she began to cry.

"What are you feeling?" the novelist asked.

"Pain..." a rushed breath of air escaped the editor.

"Another word for it?"

Gemma shook her head.

"Come on," the author teased. "Think. You sounded like such a smart girl on the phone. And Melissa had only the highest of praise for you. Can't you give me a little more to work with?"

Agony. Anguish. Misery. Torment. Woe.

The words rattled through Gemma's mind. But none of them seemed appropriate. "Pain," she said again, speaking in the lowest whisper. The one word was the most powerful she could think of. And deep within herself she realized that she wanted more. Christ, she'd get down on her knees and beg the woman to continue to wield the whip if she didn't start up the punishment again soon.

"Now, use the word in a sentence for me."

Gemma shook her head again. This was too much. The hurt flared through her entire body, yet echoing after was a thrilling pleasure. A feeling that she'd never fully known before.

"I won't continue, if you won't play my game," Jill taunted.

Of course, she could use the word in a sentence. Nothing could be simpler, really. "Please," Gemma murmured, "I need more..." but when she reached the middle of the request, she found that her lips wouldn't form the word.

"Really, now," Jill hissed at her. "You know what you have to say in order to make that wish come true."

Gemma lowered her head. Tears streaked her pretty face. "Please," she tried again. "Make it hurt more—" Jesus, why couldn't she say the word *pain?* It was a short enough word. Simple. Factual. But she understood somehow that the emphasis that one word had on her entire being was a transformation of all she'd ever believed in before.

"What do you want? Tell me."

Gemma's barriers crashed in on her, as she found the strength to say it, halting, almost stuttering, "Pain."

The beating continued immediately. Jill lined up the blows neatly on Gemma's pale skin, and when the last stroke fell, the novelist uncuffed Gemma and sat her down firmly on the bare wood floor. She took the novel, forgotten in Gemma's briefcase by the door, and spread it out around the editor. The white pages gleamed in the light.

"We'll get my thesaurus," the novelist said, "and change some of those words. Maybe I did a rushed job on this one. But I want to give you something to think about first." She reached for page one of her novel. "She wore a painfully tight necklace. Her eyes filled with pain when she looked at her Mistress. Each movement was painful for her...."

Gemma stared at her new Mistress, then shyly said, "I see what you mean. *Emphasis*."

Caged

Derek Hill

I've let her languish in her cage for about an hour; an hour since I stretched her across my lap and fingered her till she was on the very brink of orgasm, not once, not twice, but three times. I know after an hour of suffering, forbidden to come, she'll be desperate, hungry. I know that her frantic need for release will dominate her spirit, that she'll do anything—*absolutely* anything—I ask.

More importantly, she'll still be on the edge, her pussy uncomfortably swollen, her clit hard as she anticipates the fucking she so badly needs. She needs to come, I know, she needs to feel that release. To achieve it, she'll learn to sync her body with mine, to become nothing more than a set of Pavlovian responses that sucks cock on the ringing of a bell—or the buzzing of a vibrator. This, I know, ensures compliance and obedience. Though her obedience has never been in question, I like to be certain.

When I walk into the dungeon I see that she's curled up on her side, her head tucked onto one of the silken pillows. She looks up at me as I enter, her eyes bright with anticipation.

She crawls on all fours. In that position she barely fits into the cage, her ass pressed back against one side of the bars, her face close to the other. She looks up at me hungrily, desperate for my attention.

I look down at the dog bowl in the corner. There was milk-moistened cereal in it when I left her—and no spoon. Now, I see she's eaten all her food and licked her plate. She also lapped the water out of the second bowl. Her face is shiny clean from where she licked it.

"Very good," I tell her. "You ate all your food." For hard play like this, it's important to keep her nourished without breaking the spirit of her submission.

She nods, knowing she's not allowed to speak. She's permitted moans, gasps, whimpers. She's allowed moans of pleasure, protestation, desire; gasps of shock, hunger, need; whimpers of fear and desperation. This is the language of a slave, more articulate than any plea for mercy or ritual of supplication. More articulate than a prayer.

I unzip my leather pants, take my cock out, and crouch down to place it close to the bars.

She opens her mouth, eagerly awaiting it.

"Not yet," I tell her, and tuck my cock away. Disappointed, she shrinks back further into the cage. I go to the toy box and take out the small leather harness, a dildo, butt plug, and lube. She remains on her hands and knees, her ass pressed up against the bars, as I thread the harness through the bars and buckle it first around her waist and then around her crotch, the thick leather strap leading from back to front. There are two big metal rings with snaps, each strategically positioned—one over her cunt, the other over her ass. She shuts her eyes and moans softly as I push the dildo home, filling her pussy. She's very, very wet—not that I expected any different. I've trained her well. I fit the base of the dildo into the metal ring and snap shut the strap that holds it. Then I squeeze a bit of lube onto the tip of the butt plug and spread her smooth cheeks with my fingers. When I push the butt plug in, she gasps—no doubt it's much thicker than she was expecting.

I snap the butt plug into the harness, too. I've got a new toy for her tonight, and I anticipate it entertaining us both very much.

There's a tiny pouch in the strap of the harness—right over the place where her clit rests—its metal ring rubbing the leather strap. I know she can come that way, just rubbing against it—the harness is just tight enough to rub her the right way. But this time, I want to be in control of her pleasure. I slide the tiny vibrator under the strap, hooking it onto the pouch so it will stay put—right over her clitoris. She groans softly in pleasure as the firmness of it pushes against her clit. I leave the vibrator off for now—I want to catch her off guard.

"All right," I say, coming around the side of the cage. "Now."

I unzip my leather pants again and take my cock out, and I see the eagerness in her eyes as she opens her mouth wide to await my cock's being shoved through the bars. I hold up the tiny remote control and show it to her; her eyes swim with confusion in the split second before I press the button.

Then she understands, as intense sensations flood through her clit, a faint buzzing sound emanating from her crotch.

Moaning, she clamps her mouth shut and shivers all over, her naked body twisting with sensation. I tuck a pillow under my knees and push my cock between the bars, reaching my hand through to grab her hair and guide her face onto my cock.

She's so distracted by the sensations in her clit that she has some trouble getting started, but when her lips begin to slide up and down my shaft I know she's found her rhythm. She takes me into her throat, her lips clamped tight around my base. I turn the vibrator higher, feeling her throat tighten around my cock as she bobs up and down. She clutches the bars of her cage, whimpering as my hips meet the thrusts of her face. I fuck her slowly as I increase the intensity of the vibrator, knowing that because her ass and pussy are stuffed so full it's going to be very easy for her to come.

I see her pushing back against the bars of the cage, slamming her ass into it, forcing the butt plug and dildo simultaneously into her. She sinks into a mindless reverie of pleasure, sucking my cock as I toy with her—turning the vibrator up, then down, then stopping it altogether to coax a moan of disappointment from her throat as she keeps sucking my cock. Then turning it back on and feeling her shudder all over.

I'm close—she knows how to suck me off just right. I'm going to come in her mouth, and it takes quite a bit of doing for me to gauge the movements of her body, gauge the sounds of her moans. They're so muffled by the thickness of my cock in her throat, I almost can't tell when she's about to come. But when she edges close, right on the precipice, I turn off the vibrator.

She pushes back against the bars, forcing the dildo and butt plug into her hard.

"Stop," I tell her. "Hold still. Keep sucking me."

With obvious difficulty, she obeys. She keeps sucking me off, her head the only part of her that's moving. I keep her immobile until I'm so close that I know I can come at any moment.

"Now," I say. "Fuck yourself."

I turn the vibrator on its highest setting and listen to her shriek deep in her filled throat, watch her hips piston back, slamming her ass violently against the bars, fucking the dildo and butt plug simultaneously into her. I don't let myself go until I hear her groan, then grunt, then see her pound once, twice, three times harder than ever before against the bars, and I know she's coming. My hips pump fast against her, forcing my cock into her mouth just shallow enough so that when I come, I spurt my whole thick load into her mouth. She sucks hungrily, her hips shaking from orgasm as she swallows it all. She slumps, exhausted, against the bars and I turn off the vibrator, pulling my cock out of her come-dripping mouth.

I reach through the bars and caress her face, looking down at it all slick. I smile at her.

She asked for this—to be taught to come when I shoot in her mouth. For her it's the pinnacle of submission: To climax when her master lets himself go, filling her mouth with his sperm. I don't know if Pavlov would approve, but I think after a few dozen more times like this, her mouth will start to water whenever she hears that buzzing sound. Someday, perhaps, the vibrator and dildos will be gone—and she'll come just from the taste of my semen, flooding her mouth, gushing thick down her throat.

Physiologically impossible? Perhaps. But she dreams, as I do, that physiology is only the smallest part of a slave girl's orgasm.

Six Persimmons

Helena Settimana

He had bitten and suckled at her nipples until they were raw and tender and resembled overripe raspberries. Her legs were bent back at the knees; her feet splayed out beside her. Her back arched tightly away from her hips; her hands, bound together, were anchored above her head. At that moment, he traced the centerline of her body, dragging the nail of one finger edgewise toward the cleft which marked the divide of her pubis. She looked radiant. Her hips rose.

He found her in a bar in Tokyo—a bar with a decidedly Henry Miller–esque name. It was the sort of place that *gaijin* went to, seeking the familiar and the exotic. She sat alone, a slightly taller than average woman with coltish legs and chestnut hair. It was coarse in texture, like a mare's tail. She wore a simple baby blue-silk dress and looked about fifteen, but when he asked her age, she said twenty-five, and he decided she must be thirty. A woman in Tokyo never claims to be older than she is. Still, she had a young face, with eyes almost too large, which accentuated the illusion of extreme youth. Her nose was lightly dusted with freckles but otherwise hers was very creamy, very fine, alabaster skin. She looked both Japanese and Western at the same time.

He sent her a drink, which she accepted without acknowledgment. The man bore disdain poorly. Her disinterest aggravated him as the minutes passed and he moved quietly toward her until he stood beside her, and asked politely if he could buy her another. To his surprise, rather than lowering her eyes when spoken to, she raised them to him and answered, softly, that yes, she would very much like another. He was encouraged to be direct. As she raised the second glass to her lips, he asked her, frankly, what she was like between the legs. He said simply that it interested him in an abstract sort of way, that he had two possibilities in his mind: one that she was as bald and smooth as a schoolgirl, demure and untouched; the other that she wore a mane of thick black hair as wild as the beard of a dragon in the valley between her legs. He was trying to imagine what she would be like in bed and somehow this detail would tell him all he needed to know about her.

There did not seem to be much need to negotiate. He made clear his interest, and she did not rebuff him. They danced slow and close and dangerous for a little while, and he whispered something in her ear. Then he sent for their coats.

It was an autumn night, and raining steadily. The towering buildings were gunmetal in the half-light cast by the signs everywhere. They walked a short distance, heads down; she, tottering on heels not meant to be walked upon. Water began to trickle down their necks, plastering hair to their foreheads. The quarter was shrouded in mist and the streets were like quicksilver from broken glass, greasy, reflecting the neon and streetlamps and taillights of passing cars. He hailed a cab.

He kissed her in the back of the car, teeth tearing her lips, crushing her lips, smearing the paint on them, raking over the curve of her cheekbones, scraping the arc of her neck.

Ferocious. She sank further back into the seat, not in resistance, but submission. His mouth sought her breast and pulled a nipple from its restraint. She made a sound like, "Ai," exhaled, and her hand moved slowly to the juncture of his legs, where he stopped her, held her wrist, and shook his head.

The place at which they arrived was in near darkness, and as they entered and removed their shoes, he turned on a small floor lamp in the main living area. The room was spare, but not bare: *tatami,* a futon covered in black fabric, low teak tables, a couple of chairs, an *ikebana* arrangement on a table by the window, and in the center of the room a *raku* bowl filled with shining, orange fruit.

The door clicked shut behind them. In the dim light of the room she looked far younger, more vulnerable than she had in the bar; disheveled, disarranged. The girl moved over to the window, where one of those panoramic views of the night city was laid out like spangled tapestry in the background. There was a small sill beneath the glass. She sat on it, and turned herself to face him once again. Turned herself to face him, and hiked her skirt up just a bit; just enough that he could almost see her. She said, softly, simply, "You wanted to know."

He moved across the room, pulled her hands down, pulled her dress down to cover the tops of her thighs and drew her to the center of the room, into the pool of light cast by the long-necked, arced lamp. He ordered her to stand still, and then slipped behind her. He fed upon the nape of her neck, showering it with kisses and clawing it with his teeth. She pressed back into him, and for the first time he felt his burning hardness pressed into her. He wrapped her in his arms, holding her breasts, her belly, the mount of her pubis in a firm embrace. The girl had thrown back her head, so that her still-damp hair hung down her back. He gathered it and held it up and nuzzled under it until his teeth found the pull tag of the zipper of her dress, and he slowly drew it downward until her back lay open and exposed to the junction of her spine and buttocks. He drew his tongue down the valley of her back, between her shoulder blades, and came to a stop at the cleft of her ass. Her legs were shaking. She reached for his head, to feel the shape of it, the texture of his hair, but again he dissuaded her.

Turning her around so that she faced him, he drew the dress off. It made a dry, rustling sound, like rice paper being crumpled. In the light of the one lamp she stood like an exhibit; hands, arms suddenly crossed self consciously over her breasts, atop her panties, like Aphrodite emerging from the sea. He ordered her to wait, rose from his spot kneeling upon the floor and disappeared. She could hear the hiss of the *shoji* as he left the room. She stood like a shining stone. When he reemerged, he carried a cloth bag in his hand, and wore a soberly colored man's robe, tied at the waist.

Kneeling, he drew her forward by her hips, until his nose was pressed to the fabric of her undergarments. His hands crept and twined up her legs and one, then two fingers slipped beneath the fabric. He smiled up at her. From the bag, he pulled a large hunting knife. Her breath rattled inwardly like the dry leaves of that autumn, and she stiffened slightly, but did not move.

He cut the garment from her body with such force that she cried out, and nearly fell. The man smiled. He placed the knife on the low table with the fruit, held her firmly and buried his face into her sex. She was not entirely as he had expected, but a bit of both: a luxurious thatch of hair crowned her mons, but her greater lips were smooth. He nuzzled into her, inhaling deeply and rubbing his nose firmly into the soft dampness there. She shook her head so that the red mane cascaded forward covering her face, and swept over his head and tickled his brow as she stooped over him.

"Lie down," he breathed.

The musk from her had grown quite strong and provoked his erection further. It disturbed the front of his robe. She lowered herself to the mat and stretched out beside him where he knelt.

"You have beautiful skin," he said.

The girl stared at him for a long moment.

He reached for the bag on the floor, and drew a quantity of black rope from it. "Sit up."

The girl sat. He wound the rope carefully around her ribs, drawing each loop tightly until the dark cords dug into her flesh and then about her breasts so that they stood out and began to choke with blood and darken. He bound her wrists, and then her ankles with the same deliberate intensity, pausing now and again to admire his handiwork. With an almost baroque complexity he wound the heavy cords so that they passed between her legs and around her neck, again and again, until the roundness of her vulva bulged like an overfilled cushion about to burst. She began to moan softly. He ordered her to her knees, and then down onto her elbows. He studied the effect in the light. A trickle of moisture had appeared in the cleft between her legs. It ran slowly from its source, to the knot of flesh around her clitoris. She shifted her knees and her ass shook gently as she did so. He sat behind her, the disturbance in his robe ever more noticeable.

The man reached for a piece of fruit from the bowl nearby.

"Persimmons. Their flesh is like the flesh of a woman in heat." He sat beside her, turning the vermilion fruit around in his hand.

"Look. I have six varieties here: every one has its own character, every one has its own taste, its own shape; just like a woman. Like a woman, they are not good to eat unless prepared and ripened properly. They will turn your mouth to sand if you try to hurry them. Shall you turn my tongue into a desert? No...I do not think so."

"Here is *Hanafuyu,* which is sweet but has little flavor; and here *Fuyu*, and *Gosho* and *Saijo*, *Hachiya*: Look how it is different, shaped like an acorn! And here is the best...*Hyakume*: it tastes like spice."

The girl emitted a low moan. Her ass wagged suggestively in the air, and he offered it his hand, stroking it the way an indulgent master strokes a favored pet. She pushed her hips higher. He proffered one finger, and explored the velvet ruffles of her lips, smoothing the moisture which appeared there over the entire prominence until the mound itself was shining and swollen and filled with color, peach-like. He entered her with two fingers, and then with three. The girl emitted a keening note, and pushed back upon him. He withdrew his hand. The smell was overwhelming, and his penis pitched and shook beneath his robe. Exposing it, he laid it against the soft knot of flesh she displayed, and pushed. The girl cried out and arched her back, pressing once again to meet him as he moved inside her.

He reached again for the knife. There was a dull glow, which reflected off of its edge. The fruit was ripe to bursting, a translucent sac of flesh and juice. He pulled the green calyx from the top of the orb and then began to peel it with the knife. A trickle of pale juice ran down his arm. He divided the first persimmon into quarters, then into eighths and laid the sections artfully across the hemispheres of her ass and the rounded muscles flanking her spine. He added a second and a third fruit to his display and still resting within her, stooped to pluck the bright delicacies from her back with his mouth. He knotted his hands into her hair, and pulled, drawing her head back toward his chest, exposing her bound throat, causing her mouth to open, causing her to gasp for air, causing the ropes flanking her cunt to tighten further.

"Open your mouth wider," he said, and as she did so he pulled her head to his chest and slid a tender morsel into her mouth. He rested a second piece upon her lips, and lowered himself to bite it in half urging her to meet him halfway. Their teeth clicked together. *"Hanafuyu,"* he said, and thrust himself into her so hard that the girl pulled away and emitted a sharp cry. The binding had made her unnaturally tight. He plucked another morsel from the hummock of her butt, and pulled her head back to drop it ceremoniously upon her lips. "*Fuyu,*"he breathed, and drove himself into her with force. "Do you like the *taste*? That one should *taste* better, no?"

The girl nodded and murmured, "Oh yes, better."

He withdrew from her body.

Reaching into the bag, he produced a long, wide, black silk scarf, which he deftly folded and then wrapped about her head, her eyes. He stroked her hair, and her face, which was upturned toward him. He shook his penis before her. It was a magnificent specimen, thick and pendant, and laced with prominent teal veins which fairly pulsed at their treatment. It was anchored by a dense and concentrated mat of shining black hair. He brushed her face with it. He stroked her face and her hair and left shining, silvery traces upon the smoothness of her cheeks. It rested below her nose where she could smell herself, mixed with his own scent. He touched it to her lips then lay a translucent, wet, piece of persimmon upon the glans, and proffered it once more. "*Gosho.*" he breathed, and forced the sweet fruit, piggybacking his cock, to the back of the woman's throat. He offered her one, two, three, more pieces in the same manner, rhythmically rocking himself between her lips, his face dark with concentration. He withdrew once again and pressing upon her hips managed to turn her about so that he was once again facing her ass. He loosened the bonds on her ankles and pushed her legs apart. The man peeled her lips open, exposing the mouth of her vagina; pulled on the lips, until the hole gaped and parted. He rose into a low crouch and grasped her hips with his knees to sharpen his angle of entry; to further tighten her grasp on his cock. The woman with the reddish-brown hair began to cry out softly. Her sounds rose and fell in rhythm with his thrusts, but as she drew nearer her pleasure, he stopped and once again began to divide the fruit.

"Lie down on your back," he ordered, and the woman slowly toppled to her side and struggled to roll into a supine position.

"Put your hands over your head," he said, and she once again obeyed. He looped an extra length of rope between her bound wrists, and anchored the loose ends so that her arms were now immobilized.

She lay there on the *tatami*, panting, veiled, bound. He knew her breasts ached slightly and her nipples itched. He slapped her, gently at first, and then with increasing vigor as her nipples grew erect and reddened. The woman twisted and moaned and attempted to arch her back to meet the open palm of his hand. Again the fragrance which rose from her increased, and the trickle between her legs turned to a gush. He bit her and chewed at her, stopping just short of tearing her skin, of marring it, until her nipples took on the look of overripe raspberries. She looked radiant.

The man's own face had taken on a peculiar look of concentrated rapture. He drew the nail of his index finger down the centerline of her body and her hips rose; a bright weal sprung up in its place. The man's mouth hung open, a small, pink, wet O.

The last of the fruit lay divided, except for one piece, still intact. The glistening bits he lay upon her belly and mons, which heaved and shook as he licked and bit his way southward. "The taste," he murmured, "the *taste,*" and plunged his tongue between her legs, into the deep velvet sweetness, smearing his face, his nose, his mouth with the watery, pungent essence of ripe fruit; vegetal and feminine.

The last persimmon glowed in the faint light, *Hyakume;* finer than the others. Rising at last, he carefully peeled the skin from it. Leaving it whole, he pressed it to the opening gaping between her legs, and watched intently as her flesh yielded to the pressure, her swollen sex devouring its roundness until it vanished from sight, leaving only an amber trickle seeping from within her. His eyes shone as the girl heaved her hips toward him and grew louder, more insistent in voice, like a feline queen singing her song of love.

His penis bobbed and swung before him for a moment before nuzzling into her juice and the fat rolls of her lips. The convoluted candy pink waves of their lining swallowed him up again. He had lost any attachment to decorum and propriety, clutching her waist and driving himself with a wild-eyed fury into her.

Her voice now rose to a wail that echoed around the hard edges of the room as the man grew more and more frenzied in his motion. In the blue light seeping through the windows and the glare of the single lamp, his buttocks clenched and unclenched, his hair fell forward and stuck to his forehead, matted as in the rain, sweat falling in large splashing droplets upon her abdomen, then her breasts. The girl thrashed and gasped and clutched at him as bits of the golden fruit began to fall to the *tatami* beneath her buttocks. He was barking, deep from within, “Huh, huh, huh, huh,” in rhythm with his thrusts. Suddenly, he nimbly withdrew, and kneeling over her shoulders, sprayed gold and silver, juice and jism, upon her neck, her cheeks, her mouth, her hair. “Say it,” he hissed, “Say it! The taste! The *taste*!”

Safeway

Marilyn Jaye Lewis

There's no better place on earth for a bright red 1968 Cadillac convertible than the wide-open back roads of those barren desert towns south of Reno, Nevada. Or so we thought, until we encountered all the dust. It flew up and pelted us when our wheels hit that unpaved road. It found our tongues and coated them. The dust stuck between our teeth; it stung gritty and sudden in our unprotected eyes. A desert is called a desert for a reason, we discovered. Choking and coughing, we hurriedly groped for the buttons that brought the convertible top back down and raised the electric windows.

Sheila and I were fools like that. We didn't give much thought to sand, water, wind, or the elements: We just got in a car and drove. That summer, we'd saved up enough money to keep the Cadillac filled with gas for a month as we drove cross-country and back. We had only enough money left over to eat in truck stops and sleep in the cheapest motels. You know the kind: Truckers won't stay in them for more than an hour at a time. They don't provide you with a television, or a radio, or a phone; they spend most of their paltry income just trying to keep their neon sign lit, but at least the sheets are clean and they have running water.

This was early on in my relationship with Sheila, when our idea of a vacation together was to get in the Cadillac and drive for hours along state routes or back roads, smoke cigarettes and stop for cheeseburgers, then find a cheap motel, get drunk and fuck. Then do it all over again the next day and the day after that, until we'd allegedly seen the country. But we weren't interested in checking out local color or in visiting any tourist attractions. We were content with finding the next town, the next liquor store, and the next motel room; mostly we were content with fucking.

Sheila was the first woman I'd ever taken up with who could make me feel almost petite. I'm big, but Sheila was even bigger. She stood six feet, two inches in her bare feet and weighed in at one hundred and eighty pounds. She was a strapping blue-eyed, blonde, Irish Catholic girl from the Bronx. If you go by that notion that opposites attract, then we were a very attractive pair: I was a brown-eyed brunette from Ohio, part city slicker, part hillbilly trash. I'd never stepped foot in the Bronx and she'd never been to Appalachia, where most of my favorite childhood memories had been born.

"You gotta be kidding me," Sheila had snorted when I'd raised a fuss about bringing the dildos. "We're gonna be gone an entire month!"

But I was adamant: no dildos. I had a phobia about state troopers. Just the words *state trooper* were enough to make me panic. Flashing lights, sirens, gruff men in Saigon shades. Even though I'd never received so much as a parking ticket, let alone a speeding ticket, in my entire life, I had this irrational fear of the highway patrol. Sheila and I would get pulled over, I imagined, on an obscure highway in the middle of nowhere, for no discernible reason. Our bags would be rifled and the dildos discovered. Suddenly, my hands would be cuffed painfully behind my back, and Sheila would be knocked out cold by the side of the road. Then I would be treated to a forced sexual frenzy in the back seat of Satan's patrol car, my pitiful asshole penetrated violently by a state trooper wielding my own dildo.

"That means I can't fuck you for an entire month, what kind of vacation is that?" Sheila went on. "How can I enjoy myself, see our great country and relax, if I can't watch your eyes roll up in your pretty head every night and listen to you grunt like some animal in heat?"

"Sheila, enough, man. I just don't like the idea of traveling with them, all right? We can get by on fingers and tongues for one lousy month, can't we?"

Well, it turned out we couldn't, but we were too far from the East Coast to find an adult toy store by the time we'd realized it wasn't going to work. After a week and a half on the road, Sheila and I finally pulled into endless, wide-open Nevada in the late evening. We'd had enough of vanilla fucking and I, in particular, was squirming for something a little more fulfilling.

That's when we discovered the Safeway. It was a twenty-four-hour supermarket: a brightly-lit haven for slot machines, miles of beverages and great slabs of beef. It was stocked with enough Hostess Ho Hos to feed an army; family-sized bags of Cheetos spilled out of its display racks. But best of all, as far as we were concerned: It had produce; farm-fresh produce in vivid hues, unlike anything we'd seen in Manhattan markets; produce hydrated every fifteen minutes by a gossamer-like mist that showered down gently from the top of the display case. It was enough to make us stare in awe—and get ideas.

"Isn't Nevada the site of all those atomic accidents in the movies?" Sheila mused, marveling at the enormity of the vegetables. "You know, where those giant grasshoppers ate Peter Graves?"

"I think so," I answered dreamily, eyeing the phallic cucumbers and a mound of huge, leafy carrots. "Have you ever seen a carrot this—"

"*Clean?*" Sheila interjected.

Well, I wasn't going to say clean, but she was right about it, nonetheless.

When another gentle shower misted the colorful vegetables, Sheila looked at the huge, wet, glistening carrots and then back at me. Our eyes locked. "Pick yourself out a nice one," she said magnanimously. "It's on me."

My clit twitched. Sheila had looked at me the same way the night in Ariel's when we'd first met. She'd offered to buy me a drink, but then had immediately stood too close and whispered unexpectedly, "Why don't you take off your panties?"

"What?" I'd responded in shock.

"Go in the bathroom and take off your panties."

For some reason her audacity hadn't repelled me. "Why?" I demanded curiously, taking a sip of the whiskey and Coke she'd paid for.

"Because," she explained with that look on her face, that look of carefully controlled and calculated lust, "I want you to misbehave, so I can take you home with me and really give you something to cry about."

Remembering, I moved closer to her now in the Safeway produce aisle. "Maybe I should get two," I said softly, thinking of the little surprises she'd had in store for me that first night, once I'd finally discarded my panties in the ladies' room at Ariel's and willfully misbehaved.

"You mean one to put up your ass and one for the front?" Sheila asked.

"Uh-huh."

A woman dressed like a rancher's wife hurriedly tossed a handful of green beans into a plastic produce bag and moved far away from us.

Sheila and I kept our mouths shut after that. She stood by silently while I selected my two carrots; large, leafy ones, with sturdy rounded tips. On the way to the checkout I stopped short.

"What is it?" Sheila whispered.

"Vaseline," I whispered back.

"You're getting to be an expensive date," she said under her breath, as we walked over to the health and beauty aisle. "You'd better be worth it."

We were near hysterics when we got back in our car in the Safeway parking lot and realized what a conspicuous picture we'd made in the checkout lane: two rather large white women in black tee shirts, black Levi's, and motorcycle boots, in the heat of the Nevada evening, buying nothing but two large carrots and a plastic tub of Vaseline.

The little mouse of a cashier had pushed her glasses up nervously on the bridge of her nose, not wanting to speak to us or make eye contact while we'd paid.

"These carrots were probably her date for Saturday night," Sheila cracked sarcastically as we drove over to our motel room. "She's devastated."

"Well, that would explain her ill-treatment of us. It wasn't contempt, just pure envy."

Our motel room was luxurious by our impoverished standards. It had the ubiquitous double bed, bedecked with a brightly colored polyester bedspread, a ladder-back chair, a rickety desk, and a total of three dim lamps with yellowing shades. The *pièce de résistance* was a side table with two bright orange vinyl-cushioned chairs.

Sheila went to the vending room for a bucket of ice and some cans of Diet Coke, I headed for the shower. The water pressure was surprisingly strong for a cheap motel in the middle of the desert. It was relaxing, so I stayed in there longer than I normally would have. When I finally emerged from the steam-filled bathroom, Sheila was hard at play with my twin dates for the evening.

"What do you think of a puppet show?" she asked, as she introduced me to Mr. and Mrs. Carrot. She had torn the leafy greens off of one of them, so that it resembled a carrot with a crew cut, though she had left the other carrot's top springy and long.

"Didn't Mr. Potato Head have a friend, Mr. Carrot," I asked, "back in the Dark Ages, when we were both wee little lasses?"

"Yeah, I think so," Sheila replied, as she fixed me a Wild Turkey and Diet Coke. "I remember a Mr. Green Pepper and a Mr. Cucumber, and I'm pretty sure there was a Mr. Carrot." She handed me my drink and lit a cigarette for herself. "Come over here and sit with me. I've been wanting to see you naked all day."

Perched on one of the vinyl-cushioned chairs, Sheila motioned for me to sit on her substantial lap. She was still completely dressed; she liked to stay dressed until the very last minute. I was fresh from my shower and completely naked. I set my drink on the table and snuggled up close to her; we kissed, her tongue swirling around and exploring my mouth.

"How can you spoil such good bourbon with that sweet shit?" she complained after kissing me and tasting the Diet Coke on my tongue. (Sheila took her bourbon neat.) "You try so hard to be a big-city girl," she added, kissing me again, "but you're just trash."

"I know."

"Only white trash mixes Coca-Cola with bourbon—hey, I was wondering, are you gonna be extra-special trashy tonight?"

"Probably," I confessed.

"Good," she sighed playfully, running her hand between my naked thighs. "You know how angry I get when you behave."

But I didn't know—I hadn't once behaved since we'd started going out. Our first night together—when we'd met in

Ariel's and I'd taken off my panties in a public place simply because she'd asked me to—was my personal milestone for misbehavior.

I let her buy me a lot of drinks that night. I drank too much, in fact, because I knew she was the kind of woman who would stay in control. But I think I was a little afraid of her, too, and I was drinking because I was nervous. She did unexpected things. When I excused myself to pee, she followed me right into the ladies' room, right into the stall, then forced her tongue between my teeth while my piss sprayed down into the porcelain bowl. She slid her fingertips between my legs and teased my clitoris while I peed; then she pressed a dripping finger to her lips and licked it. "I could drink your piss," she said softly. "You're that pretty. I think you'd better wipe yourself off and come home with me. Now."

I knew then that with a little privacy we were going to go a long way.

She let us into her apartment, flipped on one lamp, and then locked the door behind us. She tugged my hair and pulled my face up close to hers. "I have a roommate and the walls are really thin," she explained succinctly. "Can I count on you to be extra quiet?"

I nodded my head and smiled eagerly.

"I mean extra, *extra* quiet. You see this wall?" She tugged on my hair again and led me over to the far wall. I tried to suppress an urge to giggle. "On the other side of this wall is a woman who's as big as me, and she's not going to like it very much if she discovers you're here. Do you know what I mean?"

I studied the wall, which had come up very close to my face, and stole a glance at the rather unnerving expression on Sheila's face.

"I haven't exactly broken up with her yet," Sheila clarified quietly, "and technically, this is her apartment."

My bowels wrenched. *Holy shit*, I thought, *what have I gotten myself into?* I was too horny to consider going home.

"What do you think?" Sheila whispered, pushing the side of my face flush against the wall. "Can you be extra quiet?" She swept my hair aside and practically bit the nape of my neck. Then she slipped a hand under my skirt and lightly rubbed my naked ass.

The wall felt ice-cold against the side of my face. I nodded my head uneasily.

"Extra, *extra* quiet even though you know I have to punish you because you misbehaved?"

I nodded my head again, but Sheila gave my hair a tug. "I can't hear you," she whispered.

"Yes," I said softly.

"Yes, what?"

"Yes, I can be extra quiet."

She gave my hair another quick yank. "Even though..."

"Even though you have to punish me because I misbehaved."

Sheila grinned wickedly and let her hand slide up between my thighs.

I picked up my drink and took a sip as I got out of Sheila's lap. "You're a bitch, you know that?"

"Where the hell did *that* remark come from?"

I smiled at her and sat down on the bed. "I was just thinking about that first night you took me home and told me that lie about some huge angry woman sleeping in the next room who was going to want to kill me."

Sheila laughed out loud in delight. "You were so *gullible*," she said with satisfaction. "You should have seen that look of sheer terror on your face. You were scrunched up against that wall and three of my fingers were up your ass, but you were trying so hard to be quiet. You were priceless."

"Fuck you."

"Hey, let's do it again."

"Do what?" I asked guardedly.

"Something really intense where you have to shut up the whole time."

"Sheila—"

She got out of her chair and stood next to the bed, looking down at me. "Come on," she coaxed, clicking off the bedside lamp.

"Why?"

"Because I have an idea."

Against my better judgment I got off the bed. "What's your idea?" I asked uneasily.

"My idea is this," she said. She clicked off the remaining lamp and opened the motel room door. It had one of those old-fashioned aluminum screen doors, and even though it was already dark out, it was the only thing between my nudity and the outside world.

"Sheila! Close the door!"

"Come here," she said. "No one can see you."

"I don't care. Shut the door."

"Shh," she chided me. "No more noise from now on. I want you to be extra quiet."

"Sheila—"

"Hey, come on. Be quiet."

For some reason, I did as I was told. It was an understanding Sheila and I had between us: She came up with the ideas and I went along with them. "What do you want me to do?" I conceded quietly.

"Just come stand over here, in front of the door."

I let her position me right in front of the screen door. "I think I want my cocktail," I whispered.

Sheila brought it to me. "Don't worry," she said. "This motel's practically deserted, but let's pretend there are no vacancies and we have to be real quiet."

I agreed. I took a sip of my drink, the iced glass sweating in my hot little hand. I stared out the screen door into the darkness. The Nevada sky was clear, beautiful, and boundless. It seemed filled with more stars than I remembered there being. The night air had cooled considerably and a gentle breeze filtered through the screen and made me shiver. I saw two cars parked in front of two other doors, and light shone from behind the drawn venetian blinds of the occupied rooms. The main office was well lit. I could see inside it from where I was standing. The owner, a woman, was watching a small black-and-white television set.

Sheila pressed close behind me, swept aside my hair to find the nape of my neck. Her hands slipped around the front of me and tugged gently on my erect nipples. I reacted automatically, as I did every time Sheila touched me like that: My breasts arched out to meet her nimble fingers. But when she kissed the nape of my neck, I had another reaction: I arched my ass up high, as if I needed to be mounted.

My whole body squirmed under her deliberate, patient kisses. Her steady tugging on my nipples stirred the blood to my clitoris, and I could feel my entire mound becoming engorged. I pushed my ass back against the rough fabric of her Levi's.

"Oh god," I moaned softly. "Let me put down my drink."

"No," Sheila replied. She began to kiss her way across the expanse of my naked back, then down the length on my spine.

I steadied myself against the door frame with one hand. She grabbed my cheeks then, and spread them wide, letting her tongue trail lightly over the crack of my ass and down to my anus. It circled into the tiny hole, licking it tenderly, over and over.

"Jesus," I sighed. I tried to lean over slightly and set my drink on the floor.

"Hey," Sheila said sharply, smacking my ass. "I told you 'No.'"

I leaned over farther when Sheila crouched under me, her tongue dipping into my soaking vagina. I spread my legs wide apart to give her room. As her tongue worked its way closer to my clitoris, I felt her thick thumb pushing into my ass.

"Oh god," I groaned. Keeping my mouth shut while she probed my ass was the tough part, and Sheila knew it. She spread my labia open with her other hand. Her tongue poked right into my stiff clit and licked it steadily, while her thumb worked persistently at my tight anus, pushing in and out.

My face and breasts were brushing against the scratchy mesh of the cold aluminum screen door when Sheila finally eased up on my hole. "Don't move," she warned quietly. "I want you to stay right there."

She stood up.

"At least take my drink, Sheila."

"All right," she agreed, "but only because I might want to tie you to the door frame."

Was she kidding? I looked up above my head in the dark. It didn't seem possible; she was kidding.

She was back in an instant with a pair of my nylon panties. She began to bind my wrists together in front of me.

"What are you doing?"

"Shh!" She smacked my ass harder this time. "Be quiet."

I watched in awe as she lifted my bound wrists up above my head and slipped the panties through the pneumatic tube at the top of the screen door and tied me there.

"If you pull this thing loose," Sheila warned, "I'll really give you something to cry about."

I was still marveling at Sheila's inventiveness when she came back and told me to spread my legs. When I obeyed her, I felt a glob of Vaseline slicked into my asshole. I'd been so caught up in everything that I'd forgotten about the carrots. But then I felt them, both of them, their tips poised at the openings of my holes.

"Remember to be extra quiet," Sheila reminded me, her voice close to my ear. Then she pushed both of those enormous, atomic-sized carrots into me at once. Not only were they huge: They were ice-cold.

"God!" I squealed between clenched teeth.

"Shh," she said soothingly, easing both carrots out, then sliding them in deeper. She worked them in and out, picking up speed, until I couldn't help but let it happen. I spread my feet apart wider and braced myself against the pounding Sheila was giving me. I started to whimper and moan, losing myself in the lust that was overtaking me, but still trying to keep my delirium to myself.

Then, with a sick realization, I saw someone coming along the sidewalk: a woman. She seemed to be en route to the vending machines and would certainly pass our open door.

"Sheila," I whispered frantically. "Someone's coming!"

"Shut up and try to act natural," she offered, as she hid safe, and fully clothed, behind me.

I wanted to yank my hands down from the pneumatic tube and at least cover my breasts, but it was too late. Here she came. I was quiet as a mouse but it didn't help; she looked right at me.

"Hi," I chirped.

In the darkness beyond the screen door, she looked like the rancher's wife we'd repulsed at the Safeway earlier in the evening, but I knew it couldn't be true. Surely my eyes were just playing tricks on me.

Speechless, the woman hurried past us.

"Sheila, get me down from here before she comes back!" I demanded. "I mean it!"

Sheila broke out in uncontrollable laughter. Though she obliged me in my state of panic, untying my wrists, she mocked me all the while. "Hi," she kept cheeping, her imitation flawless.

When I was unbound and once again safe behind the closed door, Sheila switched on the light and lit a cigarette, still chuckling merrily over my complete embarrassment. I hollered at her: "It's not funny!"

But then I couldn't even convince myself, because it *was* funny and I had to admit it. "Oh, man," I choked in disbelief, "what were the odds of that happening? Two lousy people in this run-down motel!"

Later that night, when we had calmed down considerably, when we'd worn out not only my tender holes, but our carrots as well, Sheila and I lay next to each other in the dark.

"Where do you think we'll wind up tomorrow?" I asked.

"Let's head south to Vegas," Sheila answered.

But we only made it as far as the Safeway.

Shock Therapy

N. T. Morley

Dr. Rachel Quarry checked her makeup in a small hand mirror and reapplied her lipstick. Today was the first day of an important clinical trial that could make or break her career as a research therapist, and she wanted to make sure she looked as professional as possible. Certainly Dr. Quarry's idea of "professional" might have been considered a bit more provocative than other mental health experts would be comfortable with, but she felt it important to look her best, and she was aware, from many years of her own individual therapy, that sexuality was an important part of that. As long as she was true to herself and didn't cross that thin line between appropriate therapy and needless sexual provocation, Dr. Quarry felt quite comfortable in her choice of dress.

Therefore, her silk top was slightly lower cut and a bit tighter than perhaps another therapist would have worn. The fact that her nipples tended, when they hardened even a little bit, to show clearly through its thin, clingy material, might have given a less adventurous woman pause, as might the tightness of her silk slacks—not tight enough to show the curves of her sex, mind you, but certainly quite close to it. The four-inch heels only completed the outfit—and besides, there was quite another cause to wear such shoes, for Rachel Quarry was a mere four-foot-eleven and wanted to make sure she didn't appear diminutive in her patients' eyes.

Especially the patients she was seeing today. After years of design and study, she was finally going to try out the newest addition to her controversial full-contact therapy. Today, a new and exceedingly humanistic incarnation of that old bugbear of the mental health profession would be put into effect. Dr. Rachel Quarry was about to experiment with real-time shock therapy, a version of her own, designed from the ground up—especially for couples.

Standing and brushing her blouse to make sure it hung straight, Rachel noticed that her nipples had become quite hard and were showing evidently through the silk top. She *tsked* at herself, but clearly she was merely excited at the prospect of furthering the cause of science. It happened to her quite a lot, actually.

Rachel took her lab coat off the peg near her desk and donned it, buttoning it just low enough to leave the firm peaks of her nipples showing at the edges. After all, it wouldn't do to pretend she was less intrigued by this new therapeutic concept than she actually was—would it, now? That would hardly be, as they say, speaking her truth.

"I told you we should have looked for street parking," snapped Chastity Benoit, shooting her husband the look of a woman who has just scraped something disagreeable off her shoe. "We're fifteen minutes early. Eight dollars an hour is outrageous!"

"One-fifty an hour for couples' therapy, and you're worried about paying for parking," growled David Benoit.

Chastity scoffed. "You know damn well, David, that this was not my idea." She said her husband's first name with a disgust that rivaled the burning contempt in her eyes.

"What are you talking about? 'We're getting couples' therapy or I'm going to divorce you, David.' How does that make it *my* idea?"

Chastity stared at David with her eyes wide. "I'm not even going to dignify that with an answer," she snapped after a long pause. Then, "You're the one with intimacy problems."

"Not this again." David slapped his forehead. "Just because I don't want you to know how I'm feeling at all times or precisely what's going on in my life at every given moment, doesn't mean I have 'intimacy problems.' I've got plenty of intimacy to give you that doesn't involve how I'm feeling or what I'm doing."

Chastity rolled her eyes. "Oh, please. If you didn't have intimacy problems, I wouldn't have had to insist on couples' therapy. That makes it your idea. If we end up getting a divorce, you'd better believe I'll have my lawyer send you a bill for my half of the therapy."

"But I paid for it."

"Like that matters! You'd just better appreciate that Dr. Quarry agreed to let us into this clinical trial. Without it, I'd be asking for a divorce."

David stood up, towering over his petite wife. "And I'd be saying 'Please, please, god, yes, please!'"

"Time out! Time out! You're threatening me physically! Security! Security!"

"Ahem," said Dr. Quarry's graduate intern, Pandora. She'd been standing in the doorway throughout much of this exchange, meekly waiting for the feuding couple to notice her. She'd seen an awful lot in her two years since taking this job, but this was way beyond anything she'd ever dealt with. In the last two minutes, poor Pandora had considered every alternate career known to the human race, from stripper to used car saleswoman to proctologist to garbage collector to two-dollar crack whore, all of which seemed vastly superior to her current occupation.

"Yes, darling," smiled Chastity, beaming at Pandora, sweet as pie. "What can we do for you?"

Pandora cleared her throat before speaking, but her voice still came out as a helpless little squeak, communicating clearly exactly what the graduate student was thinking: *Don't kill me.*

"The doctor will see you now," she said.

"I can't thank you enough for admitting us to this trial, Doctor. Without it, I admit, I would feel hopeless."

"I'm glad to hear that," said Dr. Quarry, leaning back in her chair, regarding the couple across the vast expanse of her mahogany desk. "You've both read and signed the full disclosure documents I provided?"

"Forty friggin' pages of them," groaned David.

"David, don't be difficult!" shrieked Chastity. Then, smiling broadly, she turned back to Dr. Quarry. "Yes, of course we've read them. Fascinating reading, Doctor, I had no idea behavior modification was such a complicated and promising endeavor."

"I thought I'd take a moment to clarify some goals," said Dr. Quarry.

"Oh, yes, Doctor, please do," smiled Chastity.

David was curled halfway into a ball, his face a brooding mask of discontent to the point that Rachel could almost see the smoke coming out of his ears.

"David," said Dr. Quarry. "Is that acceptable to you? If we clarify some goals?"

"David, the nice woman is speaking to you," grinned Chastity, her voice mellifluous. "Perhaps you could answer."

David threw his arms up. "Fine with me," he said. "That's just fine, fine, fine with me. Let's clarify some freakin' goals."

Dr. Quarry cleared her throat. "What we're trying to achieve here is a break in your patterns of communication. If it's successful, this therapy will create an environment where you'll both be sensitized to pause and listen to each other, and to perhaps consider what you're saying before saying it, which has been an ongoing goal mentioned by you, David."

David threw his arms up again. "Fine, fine, just fine, just freakin' fine with me," he snarled.

Chastity giggled and leaned close to Dr. Quarry, flashing her that flirtatious look she used when she was trying to win the doctor over. Rachel checked herself as she felt a twinge of admiration for the young wife's sexual prowess. Chastity's eyelashes fluttered seductively.

"Now, Rachel, you and I both know that David's the one who needs to think before he speaks, isn't that right, David?"

"What the fuck ever," growled David Benoit.

"You see what I have to deal with, doctor? It's like living with a child." Chastity licked her red lips noticeably and fixed Dr. Quarry with her most disarming look of sexual abandon.

Jesus, thought Dr. Rachel Quarry, indulging in one of those unbidden thoughts that plague psychotherapists the world over. *This unlucky son-of-a-bitch is really out of his league.*

But what she said was this: "Pandora will help you undress."

The young graduate student couldn't help but take note of the striking differences in the way the two people undressed. Mrs. Benoit asked Pandora to help Mr. Benoit undress first; she wanted time to take off her makeup, since she planned to cry. When Pandora entered the dressing room and handed Mr. Benoit a white paper gown, he blushed red and waited for her to leave before taking his clothes off.

When Pandora knocked on the second dressing room, however Mrs. Benoit answered with a musical "Come in, darling." Pandora entered and saw that Mrs. Benoit had stripped down to her bra, panties and garter belt, and was applying a thick coat of cocksucker-red lipstick in the small mirror provided. She was bent so far over that Pandora could see the lips of her sex swelling visibly around the thin crotch of her thong. Mrs. Benoit glanced at Pandora and giggled. "No reason to look haggish just because my eyes will be wet, is there? Don't worry, I've done away with that pesky mascara. I'll be able to cry and cry and cry."

Oh goody, thought Pandora, handing Mrs. Benoit her white paper gown. "I'm afraid you'll have to lose it all," said Pandora. "We need you naked."

"Ooooh, I thought you'd never ask," sighed Chastity, and made such short work of her bra that Pandora didn't even have time to look away.

Holy shit, thought Pandora. *Those can't be real.*

She tried to turn and leave, but her fascination kept her riveted.

"You like them?" cooed Chastity, running her fingertips over her breasts. "There's more where that came from," she said, and quickly hooked her thong, pulling it down to her ankles and stepping out of it. She stood there, legs slightly spread, showing the young graduate student that the swelling, pink mount of her sex was shaved smooth.

"Don't you just love sexy lingerie?" giggled Chastity. "Here, darling. Here's a gift."

Chastity Benoit, a former cabaret dancer, flicked her foot up deftly and tossed the tiny scrap of material that passed as a thong into the air, straight at Pandora. Before she knew what she was doing, Pandora caught it neatly in one hand, unable to avoid noticing the fact that the white lace crotch was so wet it was dripping.

Pandora made a note on her clipboard.

"I'm sorry," she said, handing Mrs. Benoit back her panties. "We're not allowed to accept gifts from clients."

Chastity sighed. "Well I'm hardly your client, little girl, but never mind." She accepted the panties back from the young graduate student. "Do I need to take off the stockings?"

Pandora thought for a moment. Dr. Quarry had said "naked," but the configuration of the study wouldn't be adversely affected by the addition of a few scraps of see-through satin, would it?

"No," said Pandora. "The garter belt and stockings won't interfere with the..." She swallowed nervously before she could make herself say it. "Probes."

Mrs. Benoit's eyes lit up. "I love it when therapists talk dirty," she sighed.

Had she been asked, Pandora might have admitted to Dr. Quarry that she was experiencing inappropriate response to the overtures made by Mrs. Benoit. But then, that was to be expected, especially given the duties required of the poor graduate intern. Mental health is rarely a pretty matter.

She led Chastity into the trial room, a bare white-tiled room unfurnished except for a single imposing chair. This chair, however, was the centerpiece of Dr. Quarry's new form of shock therapy. Sometimes called the 'Quarry Saddle' in the therapeutic literature, it was the subject of some speculation about the ethics of full-contact therapy, not to mention speculation about Dr. Quarry's own proclivities—speculation that filled many a hotel bar during a psychological conference after the wives and more conservative attendees had gone to bed.

Made of sterile white plastic, the Quarry Saddle resembled a gynecology table more than anything else—but it was, Pandora knew from experience, infinitely more comfortable. Her inner muscles quickened and pulled tight as she suffered a fleeting memory of her own sessions in the chair, selflessly offering her body to ensure that the technique was safe and effective. She felt a vague throb deep in her pussy.

"Please lift the bottom of your gown and have a seat," said Pandora.

"Yes, ma'am," said Chastity Benoit.

She grabbed her paper gown and whipped it all the way off, standing there nude before Pandora, except for her garter belt, stockings, and high-heeled shoes.

"Oh, I'm sorry," said Chastity. "Did you say the bottom of my gown?"

"That will be fine," said Pandora. "Please have a seat."

When Chastity wriggled her bottom into the chair and settled back, she found herself leaning quite comfortably with her slightly-spread legs in the air and her bare-shaved pussy quite exposed. Pandora leaned over her and made a few adjustments to the leg support and then began to cinch the nylon straps.

"Strap me in, commander," giggled Chastity. "I'm ready for blastoff."

Pandora tightened straps that held Chastity's ankles, shins, knees, and upper thighs to the white plastic legs of the chair. Then, she instructed Chastity to lift her arms over her head and place them in the padded restraints on the high back of the chair.

"Is that necessary?" sighed Chastity. "I get the tingles sometimes in my fingertips."

"If you begin to lose circulation, please let the doctor or me know," said Pandora. "There are several things that can be done to increase it again."

"I bet," said Chastity.

Lastly, Pandora placed a padded strap just under Mrs. Benoit's full breasts, holding her firmly to the back of the chair. Mrs. Benoit gave an experimental wiggle and discovered that she was quite immobile.

Pandora depressed a hidden button and the body of the chair reclined slightly as Chastity's legs lifted higher into the air amid a comforting hum.

"Just like a dentist's chair," cooed Chastity. "Are you going to drill me, doctor?"

Exasperated, Pandora shot Chastity an evil look. "Actually, I'm not a doctor yet," she snapped, feeling her muscles tighten again as she depressed the button that began to spread Chastity Benoit's legs.

Chastity's eyes went wide as she felt her thighs separating. "Wait a minute," she gasped. "Is this part necessary?"

Pandora really should have stopped the machine at 45 degrees, but she so enjoyed seeing Chastity suspended at an improbable angle and forced to spread her legs that she let the machine tick over into a much broader angle than was, truthfully, required by the trial.

Mrs. Benoit struggled against the straps and found that she could not adjust her lower body by a single inch. She was quite fixed in her position. "Do they need to be spread this far?" she squeaked, beginning to show signs of the dismay that Pandora had anticipated.

Pandora's eyes narrowed as they roved over Mrs. Benoit's nude and vulnerable body.

"I could bring them closer together," said Pandora. "But the technique will be much less effective." She gave herself an inner reproach for lying. That really wasn't very professional of her. Perhaps she could discuss it with Dr. Quarry later.

Mrs. Benoit frowned.

"All...all right," she said.

Now came the fun part. Pandora knelt between Mrs. Benoit's spread legs and unscrewed the hinges that concealed the operative part of the shock-therapy machine. Pandora took a moment to don her rubber gloves. Mrs. Benoit watched her snap them on with an open look of fear on her face, all the flirtation gone—which only caused more difficulty, not less, deep inside young Pandora's private parts.

Something more to discuss with my therapist, Pandora thought wickedly.

Pandora looked Mrs. Benoit square in the eyes and smiled. Then she bent down again between Mrs. Benoit's splayed legs, trying hard not to notice the pungent, intoxicating scent of the older woman's pussy. Shaved as she was, Mrs. Benoit couldn't help but display every contour of her vulva to the crouching graduate intern, who noted with great interest the impressive size and telltale firmness of the older woman's clit hood, the clitoris underneath straining desperately and, Pandora suspected, painfully against the swollen sheath of flesh. Clearly Mrs. Benoit was entering into couples' therapy with a great degree of personal investment.

But if the erect clitoris hadn't exposed that fact to Pandora's clinical gaze, certainly the obvious moisture forming on the entrance to Mrs. Benoit's pussy would have done it, as would have the full, engorged nature of her hot pink labia. The sharp scent filling Pandora's nostrils and making her head swirl was but an added, enjoyable, bonus.

Pandora eased back the clean white panel to expose the probes. She noticed Mrs. Benoit straining to get a look at the equipment as Pandora adjusted it.

"Just lie back and relax," said Pandora in the soothing voice she used when dealing with psychotic patients. "I'll take care of everything."

For the first time since Pandora had known her, Mrs. Benoit was stammering. "That, ah, isn't one size fits all, ah, is it?"

"Of course not," said Pandora soothingly. "It's designed specially for you, based on the measurements I took last week, remember?"

Mrs. Benoit's face softened.

"Oh yes," she said breathily.

"But of course, as you read in your disclosure documents, the treatment requires extremely firm contact between the electrical nodules and your flesh. Which means that at first the device may feel a little larger and tighter than is comfortable."

"I, um, think I skimmed that part," said Mrs. Benoit. "How much larger?"

Pandora smiled.

"Just relax," she said. "I'll take care of everything."

Rachel normally wouldn't have helped her patients get situated in the chair, but that pesky Pandora was taking much longer than expected with Mrs. Benoit. The little slut was probably coming on to her again. Sounded like Pandora was up for a little session of behavior modification herself.

"Are you comfortable?" she asked David Benoit, noting the largeness of his erection pushing aside the paper gown. Normally inclined to be intimate only with women, Dr. Quarry nonetheless found her gaze lingering unbidden over the quite impressive length and girth of the older man's package. Dr. Quarry had certainly been around the block, but she couldn't recall having seen a member—flesh, rubber or silicone—that cast such an impressive silhouette. Dr. Quarry tried to drag her gaze away from the turgid, throbbing thing, but found her eyes returning to it again and again as she secured David Benoit in the chair. She found herself speculating on whether it would even be possible to mount such a member without causing undue harm to oneself. In particular, Dr. Quarry speculated that it would be quite unlikely for her to successfully mount such an organ, since she'd gone so many years without experiencing penetration by anything more than the occasionally finger. Certainly she would rip herself in two if she were to climb on top of it and attempt to slide the massive thing into her most secret place. Certainly she would find herself moaning in pain, shuddering with the effort, perhaps even passing out from the—

Rachel had paused in her duties, she realized, and was standing there breathing heavily as she stared, wide-eyed, at David Benoit's erect manhood. The poor man was blushing deep red, his eyes downcast.

"I'm...I'm quite sorry, Dr. Quarry," he murmured. "I don't know what's coming over me. It's not...it's not directed at you, I assure you—it's one of those, um, spontaneous, um, things—I used to get them in math class...."

"No need to worry," said Rachel, regaining her clinical composure as she reached for the rubber gloves. "It's to be expected. It's important to be fully present during therapy."

"Oh, god," whimpered Chastity Benoit. "Are you sure this is necessary?" She shut her eyes tight and moaned pathetically. "It's so big. Don't you have a smaller one?"

"Please, try to relax," sighed Pandora, crouched between the older woman's spread thighs and working the pneumatic pump that lifted the vaginal probe. "Remember, this probe is based on measurements you and I took ourselves."

"I...I think my eyes were bigger than my...my..."

"Vaginal size does vary from time to time," sighed Pandora. "But with time and sufficient lubricant, I'm sure it will fit."

"I'm not sure," gasped Chastity. "I'm not sure at all—oh!"

With an audible *pop,* the device slipped into Chastity's pussy, bringing a satisfied nod from Pandora.

"Now for the second probe?"

"Oh, god, no," moaned Mrs. Benoit. "Not both at once—" She struggled desperately against the nylon straps holding her, trying to wrest herself from the embrace of the Quarry Saddle. "Can't we continue next week?"

"It's important to push through when we encounter resistance," said Pandora, and reached underneath Mrs. Benoit to spread the woman's smooth, shapely asscheeks. The bulb of the anal probe was considerably thicker than that of the vaginal one—*Gee*, Pandora thought naughtily, *maybe I made an error in the calculations.* Certainly the reportedly necessary size of the anal probe had raised Dr. Quarry's eyebrows, but the doctor trusted her assistant implicitly. Unfortunately, the squirming and moaning of Mrs. Benoit's naked body in the chair wasn't indicating that Pandora had accurately recorded her anal diameter and elasticity.

"No," the woman gasped. "I've never! I mean, I'd never! I mean, there was that one time, but—"

The anal probe popped in to Mrs. Benoit's tight hole, and the older woman settled down to a nondisruptive routine of squirming and whimpering.

"Very good, Mrs. Benoit," said Pandora, secretly feeling a stab of guilt for the extra two inches she'd added to the required diameter of the anal probe on Mrs. Benoit's chart. "Now for the clitoral clamp."

"Please, god, anything but that."

"It's important to challenge ourselves," sighed Pandora as she gently teased Mrs. Benoit's clitoris into position with her thumb and forefinger, holding the clitoral clamp ready in her other hand. "Therapy is a safe space to do that."

"Oh, god, no," moaned David Benoit. "God, no, I've never, I mean I would never, it's disgusting, I'd never ever—well, there was that one time—oh!"

His lithe, muscled body settled down on the Quarry Saddle as Dr. Quarry checked the insertion of the anal probe into his tightly-drawn asshole. She had guessed right: Though David Benoit's measurements had indicated a very small probe would do the trick, Rachel had predicted that he was holding out on her. She'd assigned him the largest possible insertion diameter on his chart—and when it came right down to it, David Benoit had opened wide.

His cock stood at full erection, mere inches from Dr. Quarry's face as she bent down to check the angle of the anal probe. Dr. Quarry found herself wondering what it was like to suck cock. While she'd had the experience once or twice years ago, she certainly didn't make a habit of it. But something about the size, the shape, the scent of David Benoit's mammoth organ was making her mouth water, making her throat close up as she contemplated leaning forward and clamping her mouth around the head. Unethical as that would be, it would really be a small matter, just to taste his cock a little, just to run her tongue up and down on it—after all, Mr. Benoit would probably never tell, would he?

Dr. Quarry cleared her throat, took David Benoit's huge cock in her hand, and inserted the lubricated catheter.

"Fuck me," gasped Mr. Benoit, eyes wide. "What the motherfuck is that goddamn thing?" His voice squeaked as he tried to say more, but he found himself wordless as the thick shaft of the catheter settled deep into his fully erect penis.

"As you read in your disclosure documents," said Dr. Quarry, her hand lingering around the patient's turgid, impaled pole, "it's important to create a complete circuit for the electrical current. That means inserting a catheter all the way down."

"I...I think I skimmed that part," squeaked David Benoit, wriggling desperately against the nylon straps.

As Rachel looked at the helpless, writhing patient, she realized that her proximity to his cock had moistened more than her mouth. She didn't dare look down, since with pants this tight and a thong as skimpy as she liked to wear—can't have a therapist with visible panty lines, now, can we?—there was just the faintest of possibilities that a sufficient amount of moisture might ooze out of her pussy to soak through the thin material of her silk pants.

She thanked her lucky stars she'd worn dark colors.

Rachel's eyes lingered over David Benoit's throbbing cock for one long minute before she said coldly, "I think we're quite ready, Mr. Benoit."

As David Benoit moaned uncontrollably, Dr. Rachel Quarry turned and left the room, her heart pounding.

"Now," said Rachel over the intercom. "In the last session, Chastity, you were mentioning that you thought David had intimacy problems."

Shielded by a one-way mirror, Dr. Quarry sat behind a complex instrument control panel that allowed her to monitor the physiological responses of her two patients—and to administer the much-needed electrical stimulation that would render this, she didn't doubt, the most effective therapy session either one had ever experienced.

The panel between the two compartments had been raised, and the chairs rolled forward on their rails. Husband and wife faced each other, both spread, impaled and vulnerable—more vulnerable than regular therapy would allow. David Benoit's cock remained fully erect despite the catheter, and the measured reservoir at the base of Chastity Benoit's vaginal probe had collected well over a milliliter of fluid, telling Dr. Quarry that both patients were fully present as they'd agreed to be in their therapeutic contract.

"Intimacy problems," snapped Chastity. "I don't think David knows what the word *intimacy* means."

Dr. Quarry sighed sadly as her hand seized the black dial on Mrs. Benoit's side of the panel. Chastity's shrieks punctuated the writhing of her body as current poured through her pussy and ass, seizing her muscles painfully.

"I know what it means," snarled David. "It means being far the fuck away from you!"

Rachel shook her head miserably, her hand grasping David's black dial. As she turned the dial up to maximum, Mr.

Benoit experienced a level of catharsis previously undreamed of in a therapeutic session.

Chastity Benoit's breasts were heaving, her body twitching with echoes of the pain she'd just experienced.

Rachel was breathing hard, her empathy with her clients betraying itself as Pandora stood behind her, observing closely, making little notes on her clipboard.

"David, did you have something you wanted to say in response to your wife's comment?" asked Rachel, her fingertips tingling as she held them on the black dial.

"Nope," he said weakly. "Not a damn thing."

"Oh come on," said Rachel through gritted teeth. "Chastity just said she doesn't think you know what the word *intimacy* means. You must have some response for her."

Rachel gripped the black dial tightly, her lips twitching slightly in anticipation of cranking it back up to maximum.

"I think she's the one—" David Benoit began. Dr. Quarry's hand was milliseconds from offering the little rascal a full-on twist, when he blurted out: "She's the one who suffers from my difficulties at providing intimacy."

Rachel's lips turned up in a smile.

"Very good, David," she sighed, transferring her hand to the white dial. "That was a very brave thing to say." She twisted the white dial, and David began to moan softly, humping his body against the Quarry Saddle. She let him shudder there for a moment, lost in abject ecstasy as current flowed down the inside of his cock and reached the plug distending his asshole. When she ceased the current, David Benoit's mouth hung open, slack.

"Chastity," sighed Dr. Quarry. "Wasn't that a brave thing for David to admit?"

"Brave for a manipulative little—aaaaaaaaaaargh!" Chastity thrashed and writhed in the saddle as Rachel cranked the black button up to maximum and hit the switch marked "overdrive." This time, Rachel left Chastity Benoit twisting in the wind for a full minute—she was getting sick and tired of the little cunt's attitude.

Rachel killed the power and Chastity's body ceased its wild thrashing.

"I'm sorry," said Rachel pleasantly. "You were saying?"

Chastity swallowed nervously.

"Yes," she murmured. "It was a very brave thing to say, David."

"I'm sorry, I don't think I heard her," said David, his eyes perking up. "Honey, could you repeat that?"

Chastity stared at her husband with her eyebrows lowered. "You fucking heard me, you little—aaaaaaah!"

Chastity strained against the nylon straps as Rachel held her on overdrive for two long minutes. Probably longer than was clinically indicated, but the little whore was proving so resistant to treatment that some extra therapeutic attention couldn't possibly hurt, could it?

When the current stopped and Chastity went limp in the chair, Rachel didn't even have to prompt her.

"I mean, yes, yes, that was very brave," gasped Chastity Benoit tearfully. "David—" she choked back sobs. "David, that was so brave of you. Thank you for being honest."

"Very good, Chastity," cooed Rachel, her fingers caressing the white dial like the mane of a favored pet. She still felt some internal resistance to granting Chastity too much positive feedback, but she knew that was probably due to the fact that the client looked so fetching as she thrashed back and forth. Rachel knew she couldn't play favorites. She twisted the white dial up to maximum and watched with pleasure as Chastity Benoit pumped her hips in the small manner allowed her by the thick nylon straps, fucking herself desperately on the twin probes that impaled her.

"Oh god," she moaned. "I'm going to—"

"Not yet," said Rachel, her voice crackling over the intercom as she hit the bypass switch. Chastity sobbed incoherently as the current ceased. She continued to hump her lower body wildly against the chair, desperately seeking the pleasure Dr. Quarry was withholding from her. "David, what would you like to say?"

"Thank you for hearing me," David blurted eagerly. He began moaning as Rachel twisted the white dial.

"Thank you for thanking me for hearing you," gasped Mrs. Benoit.

"Dr. Frankenstein, you've created a monster," muttered Pandora.

"We'll talk about your attitude later," snapped Dr. Quarry. Pandora straightened and felt a quivering in her belly as she contemplated the discussion the two of them would have—she knew she'd been unconscionably naughty today, and Dr. Quarry no doubt had some helpful therapeutic guidance to grant the intern.

"Yes, Doctor," mewled Pandora, feeling her nipples stiffen under her lab coat.

"Thank you for thanking me for thanking you for hearing me," moaned David Benoit uncontrollably as he humped himself on the anal probe.

"Not so fast," sighed Rachel into the microphone, killing the power to them both. Chastity let out a great shuddering sob as she felt the pleasure coursing through her come to a halt just as she hovered on the brink of orgasm. Dr. Quarry knew she had the patient right where she wanted her.

"You and I talked about this. I think you have something else to tell David. You mentioned that you have concerns about his ability to be intimate, as evidenced by what you perceive as frequent silences—what you called his unwillingness to tell you how he feels. How does David's silence make you feel?"

"It makes me feel I want to thank him for hearing me hearing him," gasped Chastity, desperately straining against the nylon straps to try to fuck herself with the vaginal probe. Dr. Quarry sighed and pressed a button that caused the probe to retract slightly, and Chastity's eyes went wide as she felt it leaving her.

"No, no, no, no," she moaned. "I mean...it makes me feel unloved, I'm sorry David, it makes me feel unloved—ohhhhhh...."

Rachel cautiously nudged the dial up just a hint, not wanting to push Chastity to the point of orgasm and end the session prematurely.

"Very good, Chastity. Wasn't that brave of Chastity to admit, David?"

"Thank you for being honest," moaned David, his naked body shivering as Rachel gave him a hint of the white dial. "Thank you for thanking me for—"

"Ahem! David, we discussed earlier what causes you to withdraw like that. Would you like to tell Chastity now, while she's open to hearing it?"

Rachel watched David's body convulse, afraid for a moment that she'd pushed him too far and caused a psychotic break. His whole body tensed up; he froze, and then, all of a sudden, in a voice right out of *The Exorcist,* he spouted: "You're a filthy whore!"

Rachel sighed sadly and gave him a serious dose of the black dial, hitting overdrive three times as he shrieked.

"Please...please...please...." mewled Chastity. "Call me a whore again...."

Rachel's head snapped around and she looked at Chastity in surprise. She heard Pandora giggling behind her.

"Whore," whispered Pandora under her breath.

"Stop it!" snapped Rachel. "You and I need to discuss your professional priorities, Pandora."

"Sorry, Doctor," said Pandora, swallowing her giggles and standing erect, aware of the painful pressure of her nipples on the edge of her lab coat.

"All right...um...Chastity, I think there's a lot of truth in that statement you just made—"

"I'm a whore," Chastity moaned softly. "I'm a filthy whore.... Call me a whore.... Call me a fucking filthy whore...."

"Whore...whore...whore...whore...whore...." muttered David.

Rachel had to give them both a couple of minutes of the black dial just to shut them up.

"As I was saying," Dr. Quarry intoned in her most professional voice, "we'll get to that later, Chastity. For right now, I'd like to hear from David if there's a more productive way he could put that."

Tears were streaming down both the patients' faces. "You flirt with everyone," he gasped.

"David," said Rachel, caressing the husband's black dial but not yet activating it. "Remember what we said about using 'I' statements?"

"I feel like you're a wh—" David caught himself at the last possible instant, just as Rachel got a good grip on the black dial. She had half a mind to zap the little fucker anyway, but he quickly recovered his ground. "I mean, I feel like you flirt with everyone."

"You're speaking in absolutes, David," growled Rachel warningly.

"I'm sorry, I'm sorry. Chastity, I feel like you flirt a lot. With a lot of different people."

"Good," said Rachel. "Very brave, David. Now, how does that make you feel, Chastity?"

"Thank you for being honest," Chastity said, her voice breathless with anticipation of the pleasure she would receive in response. Rachel only turned the white dial halfway; clearly the patient was learning her lines better, but on a fundamental level had there really been any buy-in for change?

Still, Chastity moaned softly and rubbed her hips back and forth on the twin probes.

"Now, David. You expressed the sense that Chastity flirts. Now we're talking about your perceptions, David, so this isn't right or wrong. Who do you think she flirts with?"

"The mailman...the guy who sold us the Mercedes... the stewards on our last transatlantic flight...the butler...the gardener...the house painters...the blonde waitress at the Imperial...the brunette waitress at Andante Allegro...the guy who seated us at the symphony last night...the baristas at the cafe around the corner...all of them...."

"Goddamn," muttered Pandora. "It's a wonder she finds the time to yell at her fucking husband."

"I'm not going to tell you again!" hissed Rachel, and Pandora fell quiet.

David continued: "Her gynecologist...her dermatologist... her dermatology nurse...her hairstylist even though he's gay...her manicurist even though she's straight..." David paused, swallowed nervously, and continued. "And you, Dr. Quarry. And that perky little assistant of yours. Who, by the way, flirts right back."

Pandora felt her throat tightening as Rachel looked at her over her shoulder.

Pandora smiled nervously. "Counter-transference," she whispered with a wink.

Rachel turned back around. "Very good, David." She twisted David's white dial and he began to moan softly. "How does hearing that make you feel, Chastity?"

"Thank you for hearing me," she blurted, straining to press her body more firmly down onto the vaginal and anal probes. "Thank you for being brave, David, thank you—"

"Chastity," said Dr. Quarry patiently. "I asked you a question. David expressed the sense that you flirt with all those people. Now, that's a lot of people. How does hearing that from your husband make you feel?"

"I...I don't know," she whimpered.

"Do you think you flirt with them?"

"Yes, I...I guess I do.... I don't mean to, but I just...I can't help myself.... I'm just a flirt, I guess...."

"Very good, Chastity," said Rachel, speculating that perhaps the little tramp should change her name. She twisted the white dial and Chastity moaned in satisfaction. "That was very brave of you to admit. And David, how does that make you feel when Chastity flirts?"

"It depends," said David.

"What does it depend on, David?"

"Whether she's flirting with men or women."

"All right," said Rachel. "How does it make you feel when she flirts with men?" Chastity was still moaning softly and humping herself against the machine; Rachel nudged the dial down a bit but didn't turn it off, since she suspected the next words out of David Benoit's mouth would be difficult for his wife to hear.

"Rejected," said David. "Lonely."

"And if she flirts with women?"

David swallowed nervously. "Horny."

Chastity's eyes went wide. "That's disgusting!" she spat. Rachel quickly upped the black dial before she'd even turned down the white one. The resulting tremor going through Chastity's body as she wailed brought an unexpected quiver to Rachel's.

"Chastity," said Rachel. "Did you have something you wanted to say about David's reaction to your flirting?"

"Don't hurt me," said Chastity.

Clearly Rachel had gone too far with the last twist of the black dial, even if the skanky whore had, properly, deserved it.

She twisted the white dial to one-third and listened to Chastity's rising sounds of pleasure.

"It turns me on," she moaned. "I want you to be jealous."

"Very good," said Rachel. "And when you flirt with women?"

"Same thing," moaned Chastity, and Rachel gave her a three-quarter-strength dose of the white dial. "I only flirt with women to make you angry," she gasped. "I want you to care for me. I want you to be jealous! Oh, David, I'm so sorry, I've been so incons—incon—inconsid—oh, fuck, fuck, fuck, fuck, fuck!"

Rachel hit the overdrive button on the white dial and Chastity shrieked in uncontrollable orgasms.

David began howling like a child: "I love you, Chastity! I do get jealous! I want you to flirt with me, only with me, Lovey-Dovey, oh god, I love you so—"

Rachel hit David's overdrive button, too, and the man began to thrash about as he orgasmed—the electric catheter collecting his copious issue for later analysis in Dr. Quarry's lab.

"Fourteen milliliters," clucked Pandora, leaning down close to Rachel and reading the dial on the catheter controls. "Want to take a bath, Doctor?"

Rachel shot her assistant one last evil glare, wishing she could put her in the chair for one damn minute. As a matter of fact, perhaps there were some calibrations to be made....

David and Chastity were huddling together fully dressed in Rachel's office when she entered. They both choked back sobs as they whispered to each other tidings of love and devotion.

"Well," said Rachel, taking a seat. "I think we all did some really excellent work today. How are you both feeling?"

The husband and wife fell over each other in expressing undying love.

"Wow," said Rachel. "That's a new one. Last session, Chastity, you told me you fantasized about taking a giant concrete block and smashing David's head. What changed?"

"I love you, David," mewed Chastity.

"And, David? I recall not long ago you mentioned your desire to ram a cattle prod into Chastity's...um, 'filthy cunt,' I believe were the words you used, and, as I recall, um—" she paged through her notes on a yellow legal pad—"Yes, here it is, right here: You said you wanted to 'see if the bitch would tell you to pick up your fucking underwear then.'"

"Oh, god, Chastity, you're the only one for me," moaned David.

"All right then," sighed Rachel. "Sounds like you're both tired. Let's wrap up for this week."

Behind the one-way mirror, Pandora made notes on her clipboard.

"Another victory for medical science," she muttered.

Pandora actually would have ended the research session with a positive, even warm, feeling about its productivity if she hadn't needed to use the restroom as the Benoits were gathering their things. From the stalls, you could hear everything that happened in the corridor outside.

"At least I didn't insist that we park in a parking garage that costs eight dollars an hour," Pandora heard Chastity snapping.

"Excuse me? Street parking at lunchtime?" growled David. "Maybe you should flirt with the attendant and get us a discount."

"Jesus fucking Christ," murmured Pandora. "What these people need is a full-time saddle."

When Pandora returned to the office, she discovered Dr. Rachel Quarry standing there with a big leather paddle.

Pandora swallowed nervously.

"Your attitude today was deplorable," the doctor told Pandora.

"I—I don't flirt with her," the intern blurted. "I mean, I try not to—"

"But you do."

"I—I don't know, I mean...she has this effect on me—"

"I see. And your comments during the therapy session?"

"Oh, come on," laughed Pandora. "You can't tell me you didn't want to laugh your ass off at some of the things those goons were saying...."

She saw the stern look on Dr. Quarry's face, and stopped.

"Can you?" Pandora asked meekly.

Dr. Quarry tossed the leather paddle on her desk.

"As I said," Rachel smiled, "your attitude today was deplorable. But I've decided disciplinary action won't be necessary."

Pandora let out a sigh of relief.

"Thank you, Doctor," she said softly, her eyes downcast. "I promise it won't happen again."

"However," said Rachel. "I would like your assistance with another matter this afternoon."

Pandora looked up at her mentor nervously.

"Anything," she squeaked.

Rachel smiled.

"After such an extensive and productive session," said Dr. Quarry, "There are some necessary calibrations that I must perform to the chairs. I would like you to stand in as subject, since they must be performed while the chairs are occupied."

Pandora giggled nervously.

"You're joking?"

"I never joke," said Rachel.

"B...both chairs?"

"Both of them. All contact points. And a few we haven't tried out yet."

"For how long?"

"Oh, I don't know," said Rachel, her smile turning from condescension to outright evil. "Could take a couple of hours. Per chair."

"I...I...I've got a seminar," croaked Pandora.

"I've taken the liberty of canceling it," smiled Rachel. "This is more important."

"Wh...when do we...?" Pandora felt her knees quaking, staring into the cold, cruel eyes of her mentor.

Rachel lifted her eyebrows and glanced at her wristwatch.

Pandora looked down at her feet.

"You can change in the dressing room," said Rachel. "No need to bother with a gown."

Cops and Robbers

KC

I still can't take my eyes off of you. The party is packed with people wearing the most outrageous costumes I've ever seen—drag queens dolled up with yard-high bouffants, Anita Bryant spanking RuPaul with a big wooden cutting board. There are three Martha Stewarts and more fetching hookers, schoolgirls and underage coquettes than you could shake a stick at, about evenly divided between women and men in their twenties, thirties and forties.

But you're the one I can't take my eyes off, because you look like nothing I've ever expected.

You were so secretive about your costume, stashing it at work, blowing off my questions with vague smiles, giving me just the most tantalizing of hints. But I really had no idea. When you walked out of the bathroom wearing that outfit, I just about flipped. Your knee-high motorcycle boots were polished till they gleamed, and their heels added a good two inches to your already impressive height. Your tan pants fit tight and flawlessly, the dark stripe outlining your long, muscled legs. You had the helmet, too, complete with microphone.

Your belt had everything it was supposed to have: ammo cases packed with condoms, a fake gun. And handcuffs.

I could see myself in your mirrored aviator sunglasses. I could see my eyes wide, my face blushing red. And I hadn't even put my costume on yet.

I'll never know, I guess, if you dropped some hint that made me think in terms I wouldn't have otherwise thought. I'll never know if I subconsciously guessed that you were going to be the vibrant, cream of the law-enforcement crop for the costume party, and so, if I wanted to get my fondest wish, I'd better be something naughty too.

You remember those fast-food commercials from the '70s, don't you? The ones with the character who was always trying to steal hamburgers? I'm a little embarrassed that my costume was so silly, but it got lots of compliments from the big-haired drag queens, so I guess it must have worked. Besides, I'd gone out of my way to make it sexy, and I hoped it would have the desired effect on you in particular.

The cape and the hat were easy to come by. I went without the fake mustache because however cheesy I was, I wanted to be a sexy '70s icon, after all. The striped outfit was a little more difficult. I found one at a costume shop, but it fit me like a canvas sack, so I sewed my own; skintight and low-cut, it clung to every curve of my body. On any other night, it would have been almost obscene.

I guess it's just a sort of poetic justice that I'm a vegetarian.

As I sit here in the big armchair, watching the party go by, I'm quite aware that I should have used thicker material for the top. My nipples are hard from watching you. They show plainly through the striped top, which has grown damp with my sweat here in the close quarters of the costume party. The room is reasonably dark, but ultraviolet lights over by the punch bowl are igniting the fires in my white stripes, making my nipples stand out more clearly, making me feel more exposed. Some guy is trying to talk to me, leaning close, glancing from my face to my tits and back again. He's some dot-com reject with a hard-on for hamburgers, I guess. I make polite conversation, searching for you in the crowd as you sway in and out of my vision, fending off (I hope) all the svelte hookers and buxom schoolgirls trying to tempt you away from me. I steal a glimpse of you and my breath catches; I can see the rapt face of a pigtailed slut reflected in your sunglasses. I feel my pulse quickening as I watch you flirt with her. I wonder if you're thinking about taking her home with us. The guy leaning close to me asks me if I'd like to go somewhere. I tell him I'm here with someone and he falls all over himself apologizing, like I care. I smile at him, tell him I'm going to go find my friends but that it was nice to meet him.

Threading through the crowd, I am suddenly lost; I can't find you. I've been planning it since I first saw you in your outfit, but I thought I'd be able to wait until we got home. Now I know I can't wait; I've got to have you *now*.

I've been running over and over the fantasy in my mind: going up to you, putting my lips to your ear and saying "I want to turn myself in, officer."

But now I can't find you. I'm crushed by the press of bodies as an ancient '70s disco anthem comes on, remixed for a circuit party from hell. A drag queen grabs me and tries to get me to dance. I beg off, blushing, pushing her away. I feel a hand on my ass and I start to turn, not knowing if I'm going to reproach some playful queen or slap some sleazy straight boy.

Instead, I find that I can't turn, because you've got me pinned, holding my slim wrists easily in one of your big hands. I'm immobile, pulled hard up against your body, smelling the leather of your jacket as it overpowers the scent of bodies, pot and liquor.

I feel your breath hot against my neck as you growl into my ear: "I suggest you turn yourself in, ma'am."

I melt, just like that. I'm yours; you could do anything you wanted to me. But when I feel the handcuffs going around my wrists, hear you tightening them between beats of house music, that's when I really feel it start: the heat between my legs, the almost painful throb, the flood of moisture that soaks the too-thin material of my tights. God, everyone will know. Everyone will know I'm wet. It'll soak right through my tights and everyone will know how wet you make me, how bad I want you to handcuff me and fuck me so hard I scream, so hard I cry. Everyone will know.

And if anyone doesn't notice you French-walking me down the hallway, it's not because of any discretion on your part—it's because they're too lost in their own drunken gropes and coke-addled dancing to notice a straight couple locked in a heated rendition of the quintessential bondage scenario: cops and robbers.

By the time you usher me into the bedroom, I'm so wet you can probably smell me. You toss me onto the huge pile of jackets, leather and faux fur mingling against me as I wriggle in my handcuffs. Every time I feel the sharp pull of the metal against my wrists, a new wave of pleasure goes through me. Helpless, I'm helpless. I hear you lock the deadbolt.

You lean on me, hard, your hand thrust between my tightly-closed legs. But you're too strong, and your hand forces its way in there. When you run your fingers over my pussy, I know that I was right: I have soaked through my tights. I knew I should have worn underwear, panty lines or no. The tights are so wet anyone could have seen them if they'd cared to look. And maybe they did.

Your mirrored eyes flash the light of the lava lamp, and you smile. It's that smile that always melts me, but I'm already melted, reduced to a quivering pool of need here on the leather-strewn bed.

"Do you know what the punishment is for attempted theft of a hot beef injection, ma'am?"

I want to giggle, I want to, really. It's funny. But my breath catches in my throat, because now you're pressing on my cunt, working the swollen mounds of my lips, rubbing your finger on my erect clit.

"No, officer," I manage to croak. "What is the punishment?"

"Whatever I want it to be," you growl, mercilessly toying with me. I am so completely at your mercy that you could have me any way you want, and you know it. I can feel how much you know it by the firm shaft of your cock pressing through your skintight pants as you lean on me. But you're having too much fun torturing me to just take me. You've got much crueler things in mind for me.

My tights are around my ankles in an instant, and the soft boots I wore are gone in a jumble of soaked, stretchy stripes, leaving me barefoot and naked from the waist down. I try to close my thighs, but your knee is wedged between them and you force my left leg far open, then flip me over onto my belly. I'm spread, helpless. I'm open for you, unable to stop you from doing whatever you want with my pussy.

I struggle against the handcuffs, moaning softly as I await my punishment. Then I feel it.

The first open-handed blow is soft; I could have handled something much harder, and you knew it from experience. But this time it takes my breath away, because your big, broad hand doesn't connect with the sweet spot of my ass—it lands squarely on my pussy. If you'd hit me any harder, I think I would have come.

I writhe in your grasp, pushing back against your hand, lifting my ass in the air. My breasts, braless and covered only by the thin, low-cut top, rub against the faux fur and leather, my nipples so hard they send shivers through my body as they catch on buttons and zippers. You no longer need to wrestle my thighs apart; with that one blow on my cunt, you rendered me utterly unable to resist you. But you still hold me tight, reminding me that you're in control, that there's nothing I can do to stop you. And that excites me still more, making my cunt purr and pulse with desire.

You spank my pussy again, this time a little harder. With your middle finger extended slightly like that, you're stimulating my tormented clit with every blow. I hear myself whimpering like an animal, wriggling and squirming underneath you. You spank me again. I pull against the handcuffs, their pressure heightening my arousal. Again. I can feel the pleasure building inside me, coming closer and closer as I get ready to let go. You spank me again, harder still, mounting my pleasure toward orgasm without caring whether or not I want to come. You've never spanked my pussy; every other time I lay there spread in your lap and let you take your liberties with my ass, making me squirm and writhe with every blow on my sweet spot, I never felt this. Never felt this merciless rush toward orgasm, as I feel the sudden blows coming faster and faster on my pussy, making me moan, squirm, and lose control.

I throw my head back, my wrists tight in the handcuffs, and wail helplessly as I come. I can feel your cock grinding hard against my body as you spank me faster and faster, forcing my orgasm into the stratosphere. I'm practically in tears from pleasure by the time you slow and then stop, placing your warm hand on my pussy, feeling me shudder underneath you.

I'm mewling wordlessly, my capacity for communication lost as I feel the echoes of the orgasm go through my body. I'm hardly aware of that big belt being unbuckled, your big cock being slipped out of those skintight tan pants. But when I feel you mounting me, feel the thick head of your cock sliding between my swollen cunt lips, I know what's coming, and I push back desperately, forcing myself onto your cock. My ass presses against you as you slide your cock home, pushing it into me until I feel it firmly on my G-spot, bringing a moan and a gasp from me as you start to fuck me hungrily, your hands grasping my bound wrists, your hips pumping wildly. Now that I've come, I'm your prisoner, a captured criminal, and you're taking your pleasure with me, not caring if I want it. Maybe that's why I feel it coming on so quickly—my second orgasm. Maybe that's why I lift myself onto my knees, ass pressed down close to my ankles, giving me leverage to push so hard back onto you, fucking myself with your cock as you meet each thrust of my body with one of your own.

When we're making love, we rarely come at the same time. Now, though, both of us are so turned on that we couldn't stop our oncoming orgasms if we wanted to. We pound against each other, your cock throbbing deep inside me as I feel the head of it hitting my cervix. Then I'm coming, and begging you for your come, which you give me as your body tenses, then releases with a smooth round of easy thrusts into me, making me come harder as I feel your cock pulsing, filling me with your semen.

When you pull out of me, I slump forward on the pile of coats, my mouth open, drooling on a faux-fur Nehru jacket. I look back at you over my shoulder, still wanting you, feeling the ache where your cock has slipped out of me.

You smile, those mirrored eyes reflecting the slackness of my face. All resistance fucked out of me, I'm your prisoner, ready for further punishment.

"Now that makes a nice mug shot," you tell me with a mischievous smile.

Selling Point

Carl Kennedy

"And of course," said Michelle, "there's plenty of storage in the basement."

I looked at her, so prim and proper in her navy suit, the knee-length skirt shrouding her seamed nude-colored stockings, the jacket revealing just a hint of the lace at the top of her camisole. She was slim, but buxom, and she had buttoned the jacket just a little too tightly, showing the curves of her upper body. I wondered what those tits would look like out of that jacket, out of that camisole. I wondered what those hips would look like stripped of the conservative skirt. I wanted to know what those legs would look like spread around my hips as I fucked her.

"I would like to see the basement," I told her. "Would that be a problem?"

"Oh, no, of course not," she said, her pretty face lit up by a smile. "I'll take you right down there. It might be a little chilly," she said. "The heat's been off."

"I'm sure it'll warm right up," I said.

"I'm sure." Michelle was flirting with me, trying to secure the deal on this half-million-dollar house. "The basement would make an excellent gym," she said. "Once you get the heat on, of course."

"Of course," I said, following her toward the door to the basement stairs.

"Do you and your wife work out?" she asked, just a little too quickly, her voice shaking slightly as she asked the forbidden question hidden by a casual real estate agent's query.

"I'm unmarried," I said. "And I would be using the basement for other pursuits."

"Of course," she said, her face flushing as she realized that her veiled inquiry hadn't escaped the prospective buyer. She opened the basement door, flipped on the light, and led me down the long flight of wooden stairs.

"It's a thousand square feet down here," she said. "Quite useful."

The basement was empty except for the water heater and a built-in workbench. I looked at the far wall and saw the wooden panel with its single latch. Michelle stood nervously, well aware of the way my eyes were undressing her.

"What's behind the panel?" I asked.

"The panel?"

"That's a false wall," I said. "It's plywood. There must be something beyond."

She reddened, obviously embarrassed that she didn't know the answer to my question.

"I don't know, really," she said. "I never noticed it before."

"A good real estate agent should know everything about the house, shouldn't she?"

She covered her embarrassment with a girlish giggle. "I suppose so," she said. "Well," she added. "Not *everything*."

"Mind if I open it?"

"Be my guest," said Michelle.

I walked to the panel and flipped the latch. I slid the panel out of the way and revealed the darkness beyond.

"Gee," said Michelle. "I didn't even know that was there."

I reached inside the doorway and hit the button that turned on the light. Michelle walked up tentatively and peered in.

She stifled a gasp.

"My goodness," she said. "I...I guess they didn't empty it before they left. I'm...I'm really sorry, Mr. Simmons." She was getting flustered, shifting uncomfortably and shivering slightly in the chill of the basement. "I had no idea. I'm...we'll have these...these...these *things* removed right away."

I walked into the hidden room and twisted the dial of the tiny electric heater. It hummed to life, warm air blowing out. Michelle's medium-length chestnut-brown hair swayed in the hot breeze.

"I'm sorry," she repeated weakly.

"Amazing," I said, surveying the room. "Would you ever have imagined?"

"No," she said. "I...they seemed totally normal."

"Just imagine," I said. "You've got a business relationship with someone, and suddenly you discover they're...what they are."

"Yes, Mr. Simmons," said Michelle. "It's...this is really embarrassing."

"Would you have ever imagined your clients were so perverted?"

"Not at all," she said. "They seemed...they seem normal."

I walked deeper into the room, running my hand over the smoothly-sanded St. Andrew's cross, touching the manacles that hung from the top of the arms.

"Excellent construction," I said. "They spent a pretty penny having this built."

"I...I can't imagine why they didn't remove this in preparation for selling the house," said Michelle, groping for explanations. Her face was now very red.

I continued past the St. Andrew's cross and ran my hand over the leather-covered mattress. It was very hard. I touched the tie-downs of the four-poster bed built out of four-by-fours. I reached up and tugged at the pulley with its waist strap.

"They put a lot of time and trouble into this place," I said.

I walked to the smaller panel in the wall near the cross and slid it aside, revealing a recessed cabinet.

"Good Lord," I said. "They've left quite a collection."

"I...I'm really sorry, Mr. Simmons. I'll have it removed."

I ran my fingers over the array of floggers, canes and paddles. I rattled the chains of the nipple clamps and caressed the straps of the harnesses. I tested the weight of the ball gags.

"They must have known it would be a selling point," I said.

Michelle stared at me nervously, then covered her embarrassment with a giggle.

"I guess so," she said.

"What do you suppose this is?" I asked, taking a harness off its peg and holding it up.

"It looks...it looks like...well, um..." She cleared her throat. "I don't know, Mr. Simmons. I'll have it removed." I saw in her flashing blue eyes that she did, in fact, know exactly what it was.

"I'd like to try it out," I said.

Her eyes burned. She was short of breath. "Mr. Simmons?"

I gestured toward the St. Andrew's cross.

"It's a selling point, isn't it?"

"I...I suppose so," said Michelle. Then, quickly, she added: "If you...if you happened to be into that sort of thing." She nervously summoned another giggle, trying hard to imply that she wasn't, that she would never be, into that sort of awful, terrible thing.

"Yes," I said. "I'd like to try it out."

Michelle was so embarrassed now that she couldn't look me in the eye. She stared at the ground. "I...I can leave you...um..."

I shook my head. "Please, Michelle. I'll need your help in trying it out."

Michelle wrestled with her professional scruples. "I... I have another showing nearby in an hour."

"Then I imagine you'll be late," I said. I gestured toward the cross again. "Please."

Her legs quivering, Michelle walked over to the St. Andrew's cross.

"What do I do?" she asked, her voice hoarse.

"You know what to do," I said sternly.

She leaned up against the slightly inclined cross, putting her wrists over her head and spreading them.

"Very good," I said. "Now take off the jacket."

Never meeting my eyes, Michelle shrugged off her conservative navy-blue blazer. I took it from her and hung it on a nearby peg.

Her full breasts stretched the thin material of her camisole. I could see she was, indeed, wearing a bra underneath.

I took first one wrist and then the other, placing them in the padded steel restraints and clamping them shut. I shot the bolts, feeling Michelle squirm against them.

I ran my hand up the back of her leg, squeezing her ass through that conservative skirt. Michelle was breathing very hard. I unbuttoned her skirt and drew the zipper down the back. It fell in a dark pool around her ankles.

She was wearing very conservative off-white panties underneath, and an off-white garter belt clasped to her seamed stockings.

I nudged the skirt with my toe. Michelle stepped out of it and I kicked the garment across the room.

I went to the cabinet and selected a paddle. Michelle's eyes were wide as she watched me return to her.

I bent down and took hold of her ankles. Michelle did not resist as I fitted her ankles into the padded metal of the cross's built-in manacles. I could hear her breathing, mingled with the hum of the heater.

"Are you warm enough?"

"Yes," she said softly. "Quite."

When I had her restrained, I ran the paddle up the back of her bare thighs and slipped it under the waistband of her panties. She squirmed.

"This certainly is a selling point," I said, and spanked her.

She gasped and yelped, squirming against the cross and pulling at the manacles. Her breath came quicker as I spanked her again. When I hit her a third time, she moaned softly.

"Excellent workmanship," I said. "Obviously the last residents had good taste."

"Obviously," said Michelle.

I returned to the panel and took down a flogger. A moan escaped the realtor's lips as she saw it.

"A good flogging can't be performed with your shirt on," I said. "I trust that's not too expensive a camisole?"

"N...not really," she said.

I took a shimmering knife off its pegs and came up behind Michelle, running the tip of the knife over the back of her neck. She shivered. I nudged the knife under her top and swiftly cut it down the back. I slit the sleeves and pulled the shredded garment off of her, running the knife edge over her back.

"Oh, god," she moaned.

"Have you ever fucked a prospective buyer before?" I asked her.

"Before?" she breathed.

"Yes," I said. "Surely you realize you're the one in chains." I slit her bra at the back and the shoulders, and the off-white lace fell away, revealing her full, perfect tits.

She moaned again, pulling against the restraints. I put my arm around her and felt her breasts, caressing them and pinching the nipples. I grabbed her hair, which was pinned in a conservative bun, and pulled out the hairpin. My fingers tangled in her hair and I pulled her head back so that, towering over her, I could press my lips to hers, violently, demandingly. My tongue forced its way into her mouth and she quivered against me as I explored her.

"Say 'please,'" I told her when our lips parted.

Her lips moved, but no sound came out. It was all right: I could read lips.

I drew the knife slowly down her back and slit the sides of her panties. When I pulled the ruined underwear out from between her thighs, I pushed the crotch into her face. It was soaked. I tossed the shredded panties away and brought my hand down between her and the cross. I touched her cunt and found it shaved, warm, and dripping. There was a ring through her clitoral hood and three rings through each of her swollen lips.

"Playing hard to get," I whispered. "While the whole time you were hoping I'd bring you in here."

"I'm sorry," she whimpered.

"Sorry won't cut it," I told her. I stepped back, returned the knife to its pegs and took my place behind her.

"Please," she moaned.

The flogger swished through the air and Michelle's body twitched. Her moans rose in pitch as I flogged first her back, then her ass. Soon she was pressing back into the slashes of the leather tails, gasping with each strike. I reached between her legs and found her wetter than ever. She moaned as I eased two fingers inside her pussy. I pulled them out and forced my wet fingers into her mouth. She licked them obediently.

"Impertinent little realtor," I said. "Begging for a flogging. We've got to shut you up on both ends."

Michelle strained against the bonds, twisting her head so she could watch me as I selected the leather harness I'd shown her earlier, and fitted into it the very largest dildo from the recessed case. I toyed with the idea of inserting a second dildo for her, but decided she would have to provide for me somehow. I slicked up the dildo with lube from a handy bottle and walked over to her.

"Please," she begged. "That one's too big."

"I doubt it," I said, easing the dildo between her lips and forcing it in with a single thrust. Her eyes went wide and she moaned uncontrollably as I wrestled the shaft into place. I buckled the harness around her. Its designer had thoughtfully left the back quite unobstructed, leaving Michelle's pretty ass revealed—including her little rosebud. I returned for the ball gag.

"Now you can moan all you like," I said as I forced the gag into her open mouth and buckled it behind her head.

The harness and gag did nothing to quiet Michelle's pleas. If anything, freed from the need for self-control, she screamed and moaned louder. The flogger swished through the air and Michelle's back and ass were striped with angry red by the time I took down the cane.

Her eyes were very wide, now, the fear evident as I teased her cheeks open and nudged the tip of the cane into her asshole. She squirmed against it and tried to beg for mercy, but the ball gag prevented her. I gave her a single cane stroke and the sobs broke through as her lovely body, nude except for garter belt and stockings, was subjected to the most painful implement in this dungeon. Liberated from her mind's control, her body twisted in the manacles and thrust itself hard against the St. Andrew's cross.

By the time I felt my cock surging, aching, begging for that tight asshole of hers, I had left twelve parallel stripes down each side of her, from the first swell of her ass to the smooth bottoms of her upper thighs. Tears stained her face and her body was moist with sweat. I unbuckled her gag, grasped her hair, and pulled her head back, kissing her violently again, my cock grinding against her pained ass and making her whimper in pain as my suit pants abraded her freshly-administered welts.

"Are you ready to be fucked?" I growled, as I pulled my lips from hers with some difficulty. Her lips continued to work hungrily, her tongue thrust out as, famished, she sought more of my kisses.

"Yes," she whispered. "Please."

"I'm going to fuck you in the ass," I told her. "Put it up in the air for me."

I shot the bolts of the manacles, feeling Michelle slump into my grasp. I steadied her and she walked, her legs quivering, around the side of the cross to the leather-covered bed. Looking over her shoulder at me, she climbed onto the bed on her hands and knees and lifted her ass high.

"Higher," I told her. "Put it up high and beg me to fuck you."

Obediently, Michelle clawed at the leather with her hands and lowered her upper body to the mattress. Her ass rose high into the air. I could see the glittering silver of her pussy rings showing around the strap of the dildo harness. Her cheeks spread as she leaned forward. A woman's asshole had never looked so good.

"Please," she begged. "Please fuck me."

"I can't fuck you," I said. "Your cunt is stuffed full."

"Fuck me in the ass," she said. "Please."

"Spread them."

Leaning on her shoulders, her face pressed to the leather mattress, Michelle reached behind her and parted her full ass-cheeks with her fingertips, exposing her tiny asshole. Seizing the bottle of lube, I lunged for the bed, opening my pants.

"Please," she repeated in a whisper as the cold stream of lubricant drizzled into her crack. She moaned as I opened her up with my fingers, and by the time I slid my shaft into her I knew Michelle had a well-trained ass. She pushed up against me, her fingers still parting her cheeks wide for me, giving me unchecked access to her tight asshole. I reached under her and pushed the dildo more firmly into her cunt, using my hand to grind the harness against her clit. Michelle's mouth opened wide and she appeared about to scream as she pulsed toward her orgasm, but no sound came out at first. Then a strangled moan of pleasure exploded from her as I felt her asshole clenching rhythmically in orgasmic spasms around my cock. I pumped into her faster, knowing I would come any second. Just as she finished her climax, I exploded into her, filling the realtor's asshole with my come.

When I pulled my cock out of her, Michelle slumped forward, exhausted, a sheen of sweat covering her body in the now-warm dungeon.

I lay on top of her and grasped her hair, turning her head to the side so I could kiss her.

"How did you know this room was here?" she asked when I relinquished my hold on her moist lips.

"I know the seller," I told her. "Charles mentioned you were a personal...friend."

"Then I suppose you don't want to buy the place," she said sadly.

"On the contrary," I told her. "I think you've earned your commission."

"Would you like to see the upstairs?" she asked me breathlessly.

"I think you've shown me all the selling points I care about," I told her. "Let's draw up the paperwork. But leave the harness on as you do."

"Yes, Sir," she said, and I pressed my lips to hers again, violently taking her mouth as I heard those words I loved to hear. Especially from a realtor.

Hard Core

Alex Mendra

"Rope," Caroline yelled from above as she hurled one end of the climbing rope down towards me. The other end was fixed to the granite wall above. I had just finished rappelling down the rock face on my line, and we were getting ready to lower the corpse. Derrick and James were up there helping her secure the body. Even though Steve was dead, nobody wanted to see him fall the eighty-plus feet to the bottom. This was the last leg of the race. The finish line lay a few hours ahead. No more mistakes. That was the deal the remaining four of us made when we decided to go on. Standing at the base of the cliff, it was tough for me to keep my feet still. I placed my hand on the cold, jagged rock, trying to block out the mantra that was dancing inside my head: *Run like hell.* That was also the first thing Steve had said to me that morning, weeks ago, when he'd first pitched the idea.

"Run like hell. That and a little climbing, some marathon swimming, and a brisk twenty-four-hour jaunt in a sea kayak to make the finish line." His voice was smooth and calm over the phone.

I knew better, or at least I should have. What can I say now, after it's all over? What can I say in my defense? He talked me into it. The Eco-Challenge. By the time he let me off the phone I was hooked.

The rules were simple. Five people. One had to be a woman. We all had to start together and we all had to finish together. All the technical gear was provided: ropes, paddles, the works. The only thing we had to bring was our team, some serious attitude, and a check for thirty grand. Steve took care of money.

"It's an investment, Pauly," he cooed into the phone. "This team's a sure thing. When we win, you'll reimburse me the entrance fee from the million purse and we'll split the rest. Not a bad return for fifteen days' work."

Steve's balls were big, but his bank account was bigger. My years as an Army medic landed me on his budding team, but aside from experience, the only thing I could possibly invest in was lunch, and maybe some new shoes. And both had to be on special.

Rigor mortis had made it pretty easy for us to lug him the last two days. Caroline had the foresight to tuck his arms across his chest and tie his feet together before it set in. He made a tidy package. Heavy as hell though, so we tag-team carried him two at a time. The makeshift gurney Derrick built was a godsend: two long tree branches knitted together with Steve's poncho. It was a little rickety, but we only dumped him a couple of times before we got the hang of it.

"Rope!" The next line whizzed past my head and smacked the ground. "You okay down there?" Caroline sounded like a far-off deity bellowing down from the heights of Olympus. "I almost took your head off that time. Try and stay focused, okay Paul?"

Caroline had been my first reality check.

Rope and Caroline will always go together in my mind. She's a girl who knows what it means to be tied down and what it means to submit. You know what I'm saying? The type of girl who understands at her very core what giving in truly means. No phony playacting. No half-assed quality about her. Yet when *she* does it, there's power in the gesture. They probably should coin a new phrase just for her: dominant masochist. Even when someone is spanking the hell out of her round, supple asscheeks, you can tell she's in control. Doesn't make her submission any less real, though. Her tears are earned through honest pain same as anyone else's.

It took her a long time to unwind. When we played, even as I bound her in place, she would tell me how to tie her down, where to place the ropes, how to pull them tight. She wanted to be in charge, even when she was hog-tied to the bed. Yet at some point, there would always be that shift. Oh, and I'd wait for it, yearn for it. At some point, she'd look at me and realize she couldn't get free without my help. Those were the moments I lived for. Her eyes wide. Her heart beating at a quickened tempo. Her full lips parted and hungry and maybe just a little bit scared.

Outside the bedroom, we weren't much of a match as a couple. Her constant critiques of the way I dressed or the way I drove or the way I breathed became insurmountable. But when I stood over that mattress, the stripped-bare mattress, looking down at her sleek, lean form, a pleasure pulsed through me that was undeniable. I could have her any way I wanted, and she wanted it like that.

My favorite method for binding her was to use climbing ropes. I never went in for prepackaged sex toy–style gear. Climbing rope was the perfect thing to bind and bend her flexible limbs into positions that she could hold easily for long periods of time. Then my method was to get right in—and I mean *right* in—and fuck her. Spread her slippery pussy lips and fuck her hard until both of us came.

She would change when I took her like that. Her entire overly tense body would finally relax. Those were the times when she could give herself up to me. Jesus, they were the *only* times.

Maybe if she'd been a little bit more flexible on other fronts we'd have been able to stay together. Or maybe if I'd had the inclination to become some macho asshole and put her in her place outside of the bedroom. That's not my style, though, and it wasn't hers. But I still think back to those times in bed with her, twisting and turning her so that I could have at her. I still think about the way her wet pussy felt when it milked my cock. The sweet way her cunt grabbed me and pulled me, as if telling me something with her body that she could never say with her voice.

I've met plenty of girls who are overly willing to get across my lap and have their bare asses paddled. Vixens who want nothing more than to lie meekly on my mattress with their fine-boned wrists cuffed together. But Caroline ruined me. I liked how difficult it was for her to submit, yet I loved how she found the power within herself to give up. If submission comes easily, then I'm not interested.

Put up a fight—even one that's only on the inside—show me that this whole big thing is difficult for you, and I'm yours. Make me work to own you. That's what I want. And it's all Caroline's fault. The bitch.

I found out she was on the team the day after Steve called. He did his best to quench my concerns. Sure, she was more than qualified. Expert big-wall climber, marathoner, and a serious swimmer since grade school. Kayaking, her only weak spot, was no big deal. What's there to know? Put the paddle in the water, stroke, take it out. One day's practice on the open sea and we'd *all* be experts. Still, a dull nagging ache kept pulling at me from deep inside. Maybe I thought her Nordic good looks would be too distracting even after all these years—blonde hair, sweeping blue eyes, and confident nature. Then again, maybe it was because the thought of being around her and readily available ropes was going to make me want to tie her down.

"We need to come up with a name. Something cool that sets us apart." Caroline, being totally Caroline, focused on the details while I was still struggling with the big picture. Struggling with the mental image of her and me somewhere out in nature, of her naked body tied in an unusual position. Of my cock introducing her once again to the type of orgasms that shattered the two of us.

"Team America." I was thankful the phone provided a blanket to cover my apathy on the subject.

"Lame. Besides, Derrick and James are from New Zealand."

Never mind they both had been living in Los Angeles for over a decade. I was sure she was with one of them. Derrick probably. He had the kind of name she would fuck.

"Listen, Paul, see what you can dream up by first practice. Something daring. You're going love James and Derrick. They're your kind of guys." As I hung up the phone I wondered what type of guys she thought I liked.

Our first practice was out in the high desert near the California/Nevada border. Steve had to fly in from his Manhattan life, and Caroline and the wonder boys lived nearby in L.A. All I had to do was swoop down from Seattle.

Caroline had to be the top dog. She had to win every time. Was I the only one who knew that within her was the desire to give it all up? To bend over and take it. To be punished and disciplined. Used and abused. Maybe so, but that was okay—because I was just the guy to do those things to her.

Pull her haughty little ass over my lap and warm it fiercely with the smarting strokes of my firm, hearty hand. Slip a loose knot around her wrists while she was sleeping and pull it tight just as she started to stir. Fuck her before she even knew what was going on. Take her in the middle of a dream, when she was hazy and soft, her most feminine moments. Christ, could she be lovely when she came. Her long lashes fluttering. Her breathing sweet and soft.

See? We fit together sexually. It was our relationship elsewhere that sabotaged the sex.

What I don't know now is whether I agreed to stay with this stupid thing because of her. Once I knew she was in, could I let her know I was out? Out of my head with wanting her again. Out of my mind with images of us together.

This dead body thing was twisted. Nothing in my past even approached it. The closest I ever came to doing something this messed up—and it really wasn't even *that* close—was when I started playing with fire. I got my hands on Dad's shiny, silver Zippo lighter when I was seven. The kind with the flip-up lid that made that awesome metallic click when you flicked it open. "Windproof" was how they advertised it, though there was no need for that particular trait in our garage. With all the doors closed there wasn't a puff of a breeze. I remember frantically stuffing one of our two metal trash cans with all the old newspapers we had lying around the house.

Click.

I had never lit anything on fire before. The speed of the flames spreading rocked my little seven-year-old mind. What started out as a tiny spark sprouting from a single folded newspaper quickly leaped into searing heat and thick black smoke. Even at that young age, I knew my impish creation was beyond my control and there was only one solution.

Run like hell.

There it was again. My mantra of the moment. This whole deal was like one foul-smelling dream. Such a simple screwup, and someone got killed. It wasn't like we didn't know what to do. Steve had marched us through our paces during practice, getting us in competitive shape, and now we were doing all we could to drag his dead ass across the finish line and win. Our team was so far ahead of the rest of them. Everything would be fine, so long as we kept the story straight.

"Listen up," Steve barked on the first day of training, "we've got two weeks to pull this thing together. That means no slacking off, no pissing and moaning, and most of all no 'I am an individual' crap. Teamwork, people. Pure and true. Caroline's gonna run down the schedule, then we get to it."

Steve never ceased to amaze me. He was chameleon man. Standing in that mid-morning desert sun, he looked the part of the rugged outdoorsman. The brown and green hiking boots he wore made him look taller than his normal six feet, three inches. A blue bandanna wrapped tight around his scalp covered what we all had been shocked to discover that first morning. He had shaved his head. Totally bald. No more shaggy red hair. The cue ball mountain man. Mild-mannered Manhattan executive turned rabid Eco-race dog.

"All we've got is thirteen days, including today. On the afternoon of the fourteenth day we ship out for down under." Caroline was sounding as militant as Steve. At first, I thought they were both taking this training thing too far. "Once in country we'll have only four days to shake off the jet lag, acclimatize, and do a systems check on all our gear. Midnight of that fourth day is when the first team begins the race."

"When do we cross the go line?" Derrick had asked. He looked like shit. Or so I thought. Maybe that was only wishful thinking.

All this was covered in Steve's letter. He'd sent all of us a detailed breakdown of the rules and regulations. The start times for each team were staggered. Each team ran against its own clock and the team with the best time won. Darling Derrick should have read his homework instead of wasting precious training time. Who knows, maybe he couldn't read.

"We won't get our start time until day three in Australia." Steve glared at Derrick as he spoke.

"Anyway," Caroline continued, "Stateside training breaks out as follows: six days endurance training here. This desert is as close an approximation as we're gonna get to the Aussie outback. After that, four days in the Sierras working technical climbing, followed by three days of swimming and kayaking north of San Diego. Then we hop a flight at LAX and kick back all the way to kangaroosville. Questions?"

Of course there were questions. Nobody dared ask them. Questions like, who were we kidding? Did we think we had a rat's chance in Reykjavik of winning? What, exactly, did I need in my medical kit to be best prepared? Was Derrick going to be going down under with my ex-wife while I sat on the sidelines and watched?

And that's how we began. Things moved slowly at first. Trust is a biggie in any kind of team adventure, and trust was the one thing our little band of outlaws didn't have. Day one was a huge pain in the ass. Steve wanted to run the show, Caroline had Derrick and James going with her plan, and the only thing I wanted to do was go straight back to Seattle and inhale a double shot of espresso before crawling into bed with the remote.

Day two wasn't much better. We only got lost three times before noon. Caroline was navigating using dead reckoning instead of GPS and maps. She assured us this was the time to work it out, not when we lost our global positioning toys in the outback. We had been up and moving by three a.m., and only realized after several hours that, with a stroke of pure genius, lunch had been left behind at base camp. The bitching didn't start until nine o'clock. By eleven, ever-precious Derrick was having a good go with the gallows humor. We all reckoned Caroline would be dead if something wasn't done about lunch soon. And I quickly realized I was humping way too much shit. There is only so much you can carry on your back in the high desert when the temperature tops out at an even 100 degrees.

Four more days.

By the time we hit the Sierras, I had my gear down to a science. I pitched the sleeping bag but kept the ground roll. No extra clothes or shoes, just the barest of the bare necessities. My med bag had the usual goodies: gauze wrap, bandages, elastic for making tourniquets, and an extra special treat. Three tiny vials of morphine I'd pinched from my day job working kennel cleanup at our local doggy doc's office. Hell, if it could give Fido a decent buzz before surgery it must be good. You never know when the party might start.

By day eleven, the whole team thing was really starting to come together. A well-oiled machine we weren't, but we were close. James and I were becoming buddies, working the ropes as a duo during the climbing training. Derrick and Steve were doing a threesome thing with Lady Caroline for the third leg. It's tough climbing with an odd number. Teams of two work best, but we settled for two teams. Period. By the time we wrapped up the kayaking I was actually beginning to like Derrick. He had a great sense of humor, even if he was tapping my wife.

Yeah, wife. Can you believe we did that to each other? Can you believe we had the lack of common sense to actually tie a legal bond like a noose around each other? Crazy. Maybe we thought that the marriage would save us when nothing else could. How many other poor idiots out there have done the same?

I remember our wedding night. Savage wedding night. Carolyn, in her gossamer white nightie, and me, watching her. I knew then, as soon as she walked into the bedroom. Strange, huh? But I knew then that we wouldn't last, that we couldn't possibly. It made me feel sick inside, and the only thing that helped erase that feeling was binding my pretty new bride to the bed and fucking her. Hammering my body into hers to wipe out the feeling of total disappointment. In her and in myself.

She still had on all the frilly pastel makeup that she'd worn during the ceremony, and she looked almost like a geisha. So different from her normal, healthy, athletic good looks. She looked like a doll, and I fucked her. Fucked the living doll in her bridal finery, her limbs bent and twisted, held into place with lengths of heavy rope. There's a wedding picture for you. Something twisted to keep you up at night when all that's left of your marriage is couple of crystal ashtrays and a gravy boat.

She was tough, that girl, and she took it, and when she came, she cried.

Did she know what I knew?

Maybe.

Did she come from being fucked like that?

You bet your ass she did.

"On rappel." It was Caroline again, bringing me back to the bleak reality that had become my life. Technically, nobody was 'on rappel.' A climber yells that to the person below as a heads up, meaning 'hey, here I come, get ready.' Steve wasn't on rappel. He was more 'on dead guy being lowered.'

"On belay," I screamed hoarsely, facing the sky. The midday sun kept me from looking directly up. I felt the slack ease out of the rope as the full weight of Steve's body slid over the cliff edge and swung into the air. Caroline and the wonder twins rigged the lines so that the brunt of the weight was borne by the three of them up top. Once the corpse reached the halfway point, the balance would shift and I'd take most of the weight that was distributed through the rope running around my waist. Everything was going in slow motion, and had been since Steve died.

Two days ago might just as well have happened in another life. We were in the middle of the endurance run. The leg of the race that was smack in the middle of nowhere. The desert outback. Iron man Steve was in the lead, creating the path for us to follow. He was only several hundred yards ahead of us when he screamed. An earsplitting, high-pitched scream that lasted only a second or two. I got to him first and found him facedown and deader than shit. No pulse. Caroline started yelling for me to do something. Get out my med bag and help him. There was nothing for me to try. He wasn't getting any deader. A quick look over the body showed two deep puncture wounds mid-thigh. He'd been bitten. And whatever had bit him killed him instantly. With that little bit of news, everyone looked around nervously. Then we all grabbed him up and got out of there pronto.

Caroline came up with the idea that night. We made camp and placed Steve's body in a tent by itself. No need to feed the animals. She was the one that pointed out the not so obvious. The entire team had to cross the finish line. Nothing in the rules said we all had to be alive. Arguing against this illogic didn't last long. At the last checkpoint we had learned we had the lead, and the nearest team was a day and a half behind us. The thought of giving up the purse didn't hurt the decision process, either. So that's how it was going to be. When we crossed the finish we'd tell what happened. Steve died from a bite and we couldn't radio in because we'd lost our transmitter days before. I was the one who took the radio away from the camp that night and smashed it to bits.

It wasn't the first time I'd smashed something because of Caroline.

One afternoon, I came home to find Caroline waiting for me, naked. I looked around the room for our ropes and carabiners, the various devices that we considered sex toys. In our world, they were the only toys needed. But when I glanced around, there was nothing. I pulled open the dresser drawer by the side of the bed, searching out our stash of scarves and cuffs, only to find the drawer was empty.

She was leaving me. I caught on to that pretty quickly. I'm not always the fastest at figuring stuff out, but the look in her eyes let me know that it was over. Or, almost over, anyway. Key word: *almost*. Before she left, we were going to fuck one last time. And for this erotic escapade, there were no ropes needed. How did I know the rules? I just did. The same way I had known from the start that we weren't going to last. That nobody can keep up the intensity that we shared. Something's got to burn. Someone's got to give.

I climbed onto the mattress willingly. Nobody forced me to fuck her. A hard, brittle part broke inside of me as I moved her into the position that I desired. A part of me, an important part, tore within my chest as I spread the cheeks of her ass and spit between them. There was a polished silver mirror across from us, and I could see her face as I fucked her. She had the same look, the same expression, as when I'd tied her in the past. Now, she was holding herself in place, keeping herself in check, giving me some sort of parting gift by submitting one last time.

And—fuck her—I took it. Took it because I didn't want her to know that she'd won.

The body hit the halfway mark before I knew it, throwing me off balance. The heavy weight of the corpse pulled the rope around my waist and hurled me into the rock face. I felt the rope cut into my hands as it raced out of control. Before I even knew I had let go, the body slammed into the ground behind me.

I heard a loud "Shit!" come down from above. "What the fuck, Paul!" Caroline screamed.

There was only one thing left for me to do.

Run like hell.

The Morning After...

Alison Tyler

Outside, dawn was breaking over a quiet city. Inside, the two of us lazed in bed, both of us naked, my skin flushed all over from your love and heat. You looked at the clock—it was almost five—and said, "I still owe you dinner, you know." Your voice was light, your tone cavalier. We had planned on a nice, romantic meal the evening before—but as they say, plans change.

"You hungry?"

I wasn't. Wasn't anything but happy. But I just shrugged. I was ready, of course, to do whatever you wanted. Isn't that always the case?

"Are you up for making the drinks?" you asked next. What the hell, we'd take the day off, right? Many people start their days with a cocktail. Generally, I'm not one of them, but today was different because we hadn't gone to sleep yet. We could think of this as simply an extension of the night before. So I nodded. Why the fuck not?

Naked, I wandered into the kitchen. You were a beat behind me, wearing your robe. I slipped into the apron dangling from a hook on the wall, and I have to say that I liked the way the strings tickled my ass.

"Bloody Mary?" I asked, looking into your liquor cabinet.

You shook your head. You were in the mood for a Hemingway, and you had all the ingredients: the citrus and the maraschino and the hard liquor. You watched me measure out the correct quantity of each, watched me rotate the silver cocktail shaker, slow and steady, not fast or abrupt.

"You're turning me on," you said, your eyes focused on me. You looked at me with an odd expression, as if you were slightly disconcerted at my movements, turned on despite yourself, and unsure why.

The windows let in that magic morning glow. Everything about the moment felt surreal and dreamlike. Probably because we'd been up all night fucking, but I didn't give over to those thoughts. I just let everything happen.

You came up behind me and put your arms around my waist. I continued to do the cocktail dance, the shimmy-shimmy shake, and soon you had undone the soft fabric belt at your waist and pulled your robe off so that you were also naked, pressing your cock against my ass while I moved. I caught our reflection in the glass door of the microwave oven, and I moved slower, more seductively, not letting go of the beat.

"Keep it up," you said as you slid your cock between my thighs, moving into the wet heat of my pussy. "Don't stop."

I wasn't exactly sure what all that shaking would do to the Hemingway, but I did know what it would do to me. My pussy got wetter and wetter. You pressed your lips to my ear, crooning softly, "I like the way you move. You've got a good beat, and I can dance to it."

You started to pound into me, making up the music as you went along, finding a rhythm we could both get into and staying with it. My breathing sped up and I finally had to set the shaker down and grip hold of the cool tile countertop to steady myself. You fucked me at a more intense pace now, and I couldn't believe that I was going to come again. After all that. After coming so many times in one night. I was wrung out. My muscles were used and abused. Yet there it was. Coming, building, striving forward until I was panting and moaning your name, begging, "Please, oh, please."

"Please what?"

I didn't know what. You were doing everything I wanted, but I had the need to ask for more of it. "Please fuck me. Harder. Harder."

But you didn't. You stopped, pulled out completely, and then reached for a roll of cheesecloth from the top drawer of the kitchen cabinet. You cut off a long piece and then moved to me again, tying my wrists together and capturing me to the handle of one of the drawers. I was bound and in your power, and I loved the feeling of giving in as you brought your cock once again to the split of my body.

Then you jammed forward, ramming your cock in deeper, slamming it home and then out again and in as deep as it would go, until your hips were pressed solidly with my ass and your chest was pushed into my back. I loved the feel of your warm skin against me.

"Like this?" you murmured, your fingers on my arms again, digging in, holding me steady. Your cock now slipped out only an inch or so, only the base, leaving the head deep inside me, and then pushing right back in again.

"Is this what you like?" you asked, "the shaft?" Now you pulled out almost completely, leaving only the knobby head of your cock inside me. "Or the head?" You rubbed this back and forth, pulling entirely out to tickle my clit and then slipping it back inside. "Head?" you asked, and then slid the whole bone inside me again, "or shaft?"

I couldn't tell. I didn't know. I liked it all. I just didn't want it to stop.

It did. You expected an answer. Until you got one, you stayed entirely still, inside me but not moving. My muscles gripped onto you uselessly. It felt good to be filled, but I needed the dance steps to make me come.

"The head," I said, and you pushed it in and out, in and out, just that thick rounded portion, until I said, "I mean, the shaft," and you rocked the whole fucking thing in me to the hilt. I was nearly weeping, realizing that you wanted me to keep directing you, needing only one thing: to come. Needing that more than anything else in the world. It's amazing how consumed you can get when you're on the verge, when your partner has the patience to keep you on that verge until you think you might literally go insane.

"Head," I said, softly, pleading, and you gave me that part, again pulling out to press it against my throbbing clit, digging in so that I felt flames of heat lick up and down my body, startling contractions that made me close my eyes and grip my hands even tighter against the ridge of counter. My wrists burned from where you'd tied them together, but I could hardly feel the pain.

"Now, the shaft," you said, gracefully taking over when you realized I just might not be able to speak anymore. In and out you went, until your tool was well-slicked with the sweetness of my arousal. Until the smell of my sex scent was all around us in the kitchen, overpowering the fresh citrus fragrance of the half-made Hemingways.

"Shaft, then head," you described, making your voice match the beat of your body, and then adding a new factor into the equation, your hand coming down on the side of my thigh, giving me exactly the push I needed to get off.

When I came, you pulled out entirely and reached for a bottle of virgin olive oil. I watched you oil up the tip of your cock with it, watched you slick your tool all over with that golden liquid. You partially untied the bindings so that my wrists were still captured, but I was no longer fixed in place against the drawer.

"Bend over," you said, "we're not finished yet."

I didn't hesitate. I bent over at the waist, my palms flat on the floor, and waited. Gently, you parted the cheeks of my ass. For a moment, you did nothing, and I knew you were staring at me, observing me. In this most vulnerable position, I wished I were blindfolded, wished I were completely bound—not just my wrists, but my ankles, as well. Wished I were captured to our bed, unable to move. It was so difficult to stand there on my own, to let you hold the cheeks of my ass apart and just gaze at me. But finally, just as I thought about straightening up, about turning around, you set the head of the shaft right at my asshole, pushing, softly pushing. I swallowed hard, but did not utter a word of protest.

"Head, or shaft?" you asked, and I knew you would wait until I told you what I wanted, understood that you were testing me, that you would continue to test me forever. That there never would be a time, a moment, when I would pass.

"Head," I mumbled, chin to chest, waiting.

"Head," you echoed, pushing in, pushing just the tip of it in, then stopping.

It hurt. Even with the coating of extra-virgin olive oil, the intrusion hurt. I sighed, trying to adjust myself to the sensation. Trying and failing. You gripped into my waist, holding me, waiting ever patiently for me to ask you to continue. Don't you know me? You were sure that I would give in after a moment, tell you what I needed. But when I remained silent, you whispered, "Head or shaft?"

"Shaft," I said, despite the voices in my head that told me it would really hurt, that if I thought that first taste of anal sex was painful I hadn't felt anything yet. You grabbed the bottle of oil from the counter and poured it over my ass. Then you stepped back, pulling out of me, and liberally oiled my asshole, lubing me up with the olive oil, its fragrance all around us.

Then you put your cock where it had been before, saying, "head," as you slipped it in, and then "shaft" as you slid in the rest of the tool. I couldn't speak anymore. The feeling of being filled was too intense. I let you tell me how you were going to fuck me, listened to your words describing each action. You knew how to move. After the first stroke, it hurt less, and when you began to press in deep, the pain was obliterated by the pleasure of being filled. I'd never experienced this sensation, the embarrassment, my cheeks were flushed and felt as if they'd turned a neon pink, a fuchsia, but that feeling mixed with the ripe and undeniable urgency of your cock pushing and pulling inside my asshole.

"Head," you said, "then shaft." You spoke these words that didn't mean much, but listening to them calmed me, let me focus on the overwhelming need to come, and when you reached around to touch my clit, I thought I would climax right then. But you weren't ready to let me. Again, your hand connected with the bare skin on my thighs, and I didn't feel it. The assfucking made me numb, or almost numb to everything else.

Almost numb, I say because I could feel it as you lifted a wooden spoon, began to use that on the sides of my thighs, pausing in the action long enough to spank me. *That* I could feel, and I moaned, and you went back to stroking me between my thighs, bringing me even closer to my release. The pain worked. The pleasure worked. The oil worked. All worked together to take me closer to the edge, closer to the finish line where I would win—dirty, and naked, and sinful, but satisfied.

You tugged my clit, pinched it hard between thumb and forefinger, and as you arched forward and called out my name, I came. You made the sound of an animal behind me, that almost unearthly sound of reaching the final pleasure point that drove me over the edge with you.

After a moment, you pulled out and caught me in your arms, olive oil still on your palms. Gilding me. And after you cut my wrists free, you continued to hold me. In the light of the kitchen bulb, we looked like statues come to life, both of us coated in the golden liquid. Inhuman, majestic, fantasy turned to reality.

About the Authors

CARA BRUCE is the editor of *Best Bisexual Women's Erotica, Best Fetish Erotica*, and *Viscera*, as well as www.venusorvixen.com.

RACHEL KRAMER BUSSEL is a contributing editor at cleansheets.com and an editorial assistant at *On Our Backs*. Her writing has appeared in *The San Francisco Chronicle, Bust, Curve, DIVA, Girlfriends, On Our Backs, Playgirl*, lesbianation.com, and anthologies including *Best Lesbian Erotica 2001, Starf*cker, Faster Pussycats*, and *Tough Girls*. Visit her at www.rachelkramerbussel.com.

BECKY CHAPEL is a Los Angeles–based writer whose work has appeared in *People, Penthouse Variations, Playgirl, Eye, Zed*, and *Parenting.*

M. CHRISTIAN has written for anthologies such as *Best American Erotica, Best Gay Erotica, Best Lesbian Erotica, Best Transgendered Erotica, Best Fetish Erotica, Best of Friction, Of the Flesh*, and over 150 other books, magazines, and websites. He's the editor of over a dozen anthologies, including *Rough Stuff* (with Simon Sheppard), *Best S/M Erotica, The Burning Pen, Guilty Pleasures*, and many others. He is the author of two story collections, *Dirty Words* and *Speaking Parts*. For more information, check out www.mchristian.com.

FELIX D'ANGELO has written erotica for *Sweet Life 2* and *Good Vibrations* magazine. He currently lives in California with his very naughty girlfriend, Katrina, and their dog, Anton.

DANTE DAVIDSON is a professor in Santa Barbara, California. His short stories have appeared in *Bondage*, *Naughty Stories from A to Z*, and *Sweet Life*. With Alison Tyler, he is the coauthor of *Bondage on a Budget* and *Secrets for Great Sex After Fifty* (which he cowrote at age twenty-eight).

DEREK HILL grew up in Maryland and now makes his home in Honolulu, where he is a part-time writing teacher and security guard. His work has appeared in the zines *Night Forum, Katerina's Corner* and *Savage Dreams*.

KC is the pseudonym for a San Francisco Bay Area erotic writer who believes some things are too naughty even to use the regular pseudonym. Her work has appeared in *Sweet Life 2: Erotic Fantasies for Couples*.

CARL KENNEDY is the pseudonym of a well-known writer who occasionally dabbles in erotica to record his most exorbitant sexual adventures.

MARILYN JAYE LEWIS is the author of the erotic fiction collection *Neptune & Surf*. She won the Erotic Oscar for Writer of the Year 2001 in the UK. She is coeditor of *The*

Mammoth Book of Erotic Photography, and her upcoming novel, *The Curse of Our Profound Disorder*, was a finalist in the William Faulkner Writing Competition and a winner in the New Century Writer Awards. As webmistress, her erotic multimedia sites have won numerous awards, including induction in Playboy's Online Hall of Fame. Visit Marilyn's homepage at www.marilynjayelewis.com.

ALEX MENDRA is a writer whose plays have been produced both in Europe and in the United States. He was first runner-up in the Jim Highsmith Playwright Competition and a semifinalist in the Julie Harris Playwright Competition. His poetry has been published in *Shampoo Poetry* and *In Other Words*. His fiction has appeared in *Naughty Stories from A to Z, Volume II*.

N. T. MORLEY is the author of twenty published and forthcoming novels of erotic dominance and submission, including: *The Parlor*, *The Castle*, *The Limousine*, *The Contract*, *The Circle*, *The Appointment*, *The Nightclub*, *The Factory*, *The Institute*, *The Pyramid* and *The Window*, plus the trilogies *The Office*, *The Library*, and the forthcoming *The Hotel*. "Shock Therapy" is an unpublished sequel featuring characters and situations from *The Appointment*.

EMILIE PARIS wrote her first novel, *Valentine*, at age twenty-three. The novel is available on audiotape from Passion Press. She abridged the seventeenth-century novel *The Carnal Prayer Mat,* which won a *Publishers Weekly* best audio award in the "Sexcapades" category, for Passion Press. Her short stories have also appeared in *Naughty Stories from A to Z, Volume I* and *Volume II* and in *Sweet Life I & II*, and on www.goodvibes.com.

THOMAS S. ROCHE is a worker-owner at Good Vibrations and the author, editor or coeditor of eleven books, including three volumes of the *Noirotica* series. His forthcoming projects include *His* and *Hers*, two books of erotic stories he coauthored with Alison Tyler.

IRIS N. SCHWARTZ is a Manhattan-based fiction writer and poet whose work has appeared in such publications as *Allspice, Blue Collar Review, Ducts, Ludlow Press* and *The Pikeville Review*. Her poem "8:48" has been anthologized in *An Eye For An Eye Makes the Whole World Blind—Poets on 9/11.*

HELENA SETTIMANA lives in Toronto, Canada. Her short fiction, poetry, and essays have appeared on the Web at The Erotica Readers and Writers Association (www.erotica-readers.com), www.scarletletters.com, www.cleansheets.com and Dare Magazine. In print, her work has been featured in *Best Women's Erotica 2001* and *2002*, *Erotic Travel Tales*, *Best Bisexual Women's Erotica*, *From Porn to Poetry: Clean Sheets Celebrates the Erotic Mind*, *Prometheus Vol. 36*, *Desires*, and *Shameless: Womens' Intimate Erotica*. She has stories in *Herotica 7*, *The Mammoth Book of Best New Erotica 2002*, and *Best of the Best Meat Erotica*. When not serving deli lunches at Dominion stores, she moonlights as features editor at the Erotica Readers and Writers Association.

MITZI SZERETO is author of *Erotic Fairy Tales*, the novella *highway*, and editor of the *Erotic Travel Tales* anthologies. Her work appears in publications including *The Mammoth Book of Best New Erotica 2002*, *Wicked Words 4*, *Joyful Desires: A Compendium of Twentieth Century Erotica*, and *Proof*. As M. S. Valentine, she is the author of the erotic novels *The Martinet*, *The Captivity of Celia, Elysian Days and Nights, The Governess*, and *The Possession of Celia*. She lives in Yorkshire, England.

SAGE VIVANT is the proprietress of Custom Erotica Source, where she and a small cadre of writers have been creating tailor-made erotic fiction for individual clients since 1998. She is often a guest on numerous TV and radio shows nationwide, where she reads stories she writes for the hosts. Her work has appeared on various websites and been published in *Maxim* and *Erotica* magazines. Visit Custom Erotica Source at www.customeroticasource.com.

MARK WILLIAMS is a forty-something married Chicagoan who is versatile, if nothing else. He has written everything from promotional material for Trump Plaza in Atlantic City to sketches for the WGN-TV children's program "The Bozo Show." He's been a correspondent/researcher for *Playboy Magazine* for many years, and is a polished professional stand-up comedian, as well.

MICHELE ZIPP loves to fantasize and sometimes she blurs the line between fantasy and reality. She is the editor-in-chief of *Playgirl* magazine and has written numerous articles and exposés, and conducted interviews on many passionate subjects. She lives and plays in Brooklyn, New York, and is currently working on her first novel, *A Ponytail's Crusade*.

About the Editor

ALISON TYLER is a shy girl with a truly dirty mind. Over the past ten years, she has written more than fifteen naughty novels including *Learning to Love It*, *Strictly Confidential*, *Sweet Thing*, *Sticky Fingers*, and *Something about Workmen* (all published by Black Lace). Her novels have been translated into Japanese, Dutch, German, and Spanish. Her stories have appeared in anthologies including *Sweet Life I & II*, *Erotic Travel Tales I & II*, *Best Women's Erotica 2002 & 2003*, *Best Fetish Erotica*, and *Best Lesbian Erotica 1996* (all published by Cleis), and in *Wicked Words 4, 5, 6 & 8* (Black Lace), *Best S/M Erotica* (Black Books), and *Noirotica 3* (Black Books).

With longtime writing partner Dante Davidson, she is the coauthor of the best-selling anthology *Bondage on a Budget* (Pretty Things Press), and she edited *Naughty Stories from A to Z, Volumes I & II* (Pretty Things Press). With Thomas Roche, she is the coauthor of *His* and *Hers*, two new collections from Pretty Things Press (www.prettythingspress.com).

Ms. Tyler lives in the San Francisco Bay Area—but she misses L.A.

A ruddy drop of manly blood
The surging sea outweighs;
The world uncertain comes and goes,
The rooted lover stays.

—Ralph Waldo Emerson